SUMMER PRINCE

THE WYTH COURTS BOOK 3

JULIANA HAYGERT

COPYRIGHT

SUMMER PRINCE

He's trapped in a dark land, and she's his only hope of escape.

Locked in a vicious battle with the tyrant king, a spell is cast on Prince Varian of the Summer Court that transports him to a realm of ghastly monsters and unspeakable horrors. There, he is imprisoned by ogres and learns of a powerful witch who may hold the key to his return to Summer Court.

But this magical enchantress is far more than she appears...

After living in the beastly land for ten years, Layla holds no hope of ever returning home—until she hears whispers of the ogres' fae captive. Desperate to leave the torturous realm behind, she ventures out in hopes of achieving the impossible.

Brought together by their mutual goal of escape, Varian and Layla embark on a race against time to return to Summer Court. Battling their way through treacherous terrain, they find themselves fighting a reignited war and their growing desire for each other. Can they make it back before Varian's kingdom falls? Or will they have nothing to hold but each other has their world comes crumbling down?

Summer Prince is a standalone steamy paranormal romance with a HEA. Each book in the Wyth Courts series will feature a different couple, with a complete story, and a HEA. Suited for readers 18+ due to language and sex scenes.

AUTHOR'S NOTE

I HOPE you enjoy reading *Summer Prince*!

IF YOU WANT to know about new releases, upcoming books, giveaways, and more, don't forget to sign up for my Newsletter!

Want to see exclusive teasers, help me decide on covers, read excerpts, talk about books, etc? Then join my reader group on Facebook: Juliana's Club!

1

VARIAN

IF THIS PLACE were called purgatory, it would have been a compliment.

At the sound of heavy footsteps and dragging metal, I quickly wrapped myself in a glamour and climbed to the highest tree branch that would support my weight. I flatted my back against the rough trunk and tried to keep my breathing slow and steady.

No sudden movements, no sounds.

It didn't take three seconds for the monsters to show up. Five creatures almost twice as tall as I was, broad and strong, with thick, rough, greenish skin. Muscles and dark veins corded their long arms and legs. Most were bald, but these five had a few patches of black hair on their large heads. Their dark eyes were sunk in, their noses too large, and their mouths crooked. Their long and sharp teeth could easily cut through flesh—I knew that from experience. They walked with a drunken gait, but they weren't drunk. And they were more agile than it seemed—yeah, experience.

I rubbed my shoulder, where a scar marked my skin. I didn't know how I hadn't died of infection, but somehow, I had survived.

Sometimes I wished I hadn't.

The monsters trudged forward, carrying their steel maces, dragging them on the earth, and leaving dents in the soft ground.

When they were about thirty yards past my hiding spot, I exhaled a deep breath.

One of the creatures stopped.

I stilled and checked my glamour. I was mostly sure my fae glamours worked on them. But right now, as the creature's eyes scanned the trees, the dark bushes, the ground, I wondered if it would find me. He sniffed the air.

That I had learned quickly. These monsters had a superior sense of smell; most of the monsters here did. I often spread mud over my arms, legs, neck, and face, hoping it would be enough to disguise my scent.

After six tense seconds, the monster huffed and lumbered after its companions.

I didn't dare move for another full minute.

When they were out of sight, I jumped from the tree branch and landed on the wet ground, burying my boots to the ankle in mud. I let out a long sigh. From nearby bushes, I fished out the rabbit I had killed moments before the creatures appeared, and then made my way back to my camp.

My camp was a hollowed-out tree trunk. There was only one entrance, which I covered at night with a panel I had made of thick pine branches.

Most nights, I slept seated against the panel, keeping it in place against the many creatures that prowled the night, creatures I had never seen before in my entire life, and that would tear off my head in three seconds flat.

I set up the few branches I had tied together to make up a kind of grill, and bunched up some firewood underneath it. I tied the rabbit—it wasn't really a rabbit and it certainly didn't taste like one, but I had no idea what to call it—to a sturdier branch and placed it over the firewood. Then, I pointed my finger at it and a jet of flames flew from my fingertip, igniting the firewood.

I sat in front of my dinner and stared at the fire.

I had been sent here through that blazing portal by that scorching witch over three weeks ago. I thought I lost a day or two, trying to situate myself and running and hiding from the monsters who plagued this strange and dark land, but after that, I started counting the days. I wanted to know how long I was here.

I refused, though, to believe I would stay here forever. Just because I had already roamed this swamp for days on end, and never found anything, didn't mean there wasn't some kind of civilization out there. Intelligent beings, capable beings, beings who would help me get back to my realm.

I had to hope there was a way, that I would find a way ...

My chest tightened and I pressed a hand over my heart. I took a deep breath and focused. I wouldn't fall into despair now. I had survived three weeks here, I would survive more, and I would find a way home. I had to, because the last time I had seen my mother, the queen of the Summer Court, she had been hit with magic by the witch Sanna, and it didn't look good.

I had no idea if Sanna had killed everyone, if Vasant had won that battle, or if my mother was alive.

I hurt for her and my kingdom. If my mother died and I

wasn't there ... there was no one else to rule the Summer Court. Mahaeru was sure to interfere and appoint someone else, but would that be enough? I feared rebels would rise up and a civil war would erupt.

Anything could happen, and I wasn't there to help. To fix it.

Time passed while my thoughts took me away from this terrible land and filled me with anxiety over the situation I was in. The rabbit roasted, its smell reaching my nose. The first time I cooked it, the poignant scent of rubber had turned me off and I hadn't eaten it. But the next day, I was too famished to care. Now, I didn't even notice it anymore.

With a piece of wood I had sharpened against a rock, I cut a piece of meat from its leg and shoved it in my mouth.

The snap of a twig sounded in the distance and I stilled. What the blazes was that? Few monsters came this way, not at this time of the day at least. I glanced to the sky, trying to see the suns from between the sparse copse of trees; they burned high in the sky, which meant it was around midday.

The crunch of feet in the dried grass reached my ears. I swallowed the meat and with a wave of my hand put the fire away. I picked up the branches that made up my grill and pushed everything inside my tree trunk.

Then, I glamoured myself and hid. I hadn't had time to put the panel over the hole in the trunk, but I scooted to the back and held my breath, hoping they wouldn't hear or smell me.

The monsters stepped into my small corner of trees and stopped. I spied them through a tiny crack in the tree trunk, praying to the gods of Wyth to help me once more.

One of them said something in a language I couldn't

understand, his voice deep and rough. He pointed to the smoking firewood on the ground.

Blaze, I had forgotten to clean that up too.

They sniffed the air. A second later, one of them pointed to my tree and said something. The others responded.

Three of the seven monsters advanced on the tree's hole.

I clenched my fist and called to my fire, knowing there was no way out of this other than fighting. Me against seven of them? It wouldn't be pretty, but I wouldn't go down without a fight.

One of the monsters knelt in front of the trunk's entrance and looked inside. A nasty scar cut from his forehead to his cheek, and that eye was all white, giving me a ghostly vibe. Even so, he looked around, reaching in with his big, clumsy hand and sharp nails since he was too big to come inside.

I sucked in my stomach, trying to make myself smaller, but I knew this was a lost cause.

When his hand, in the shape of a claw, scratched against the sack containing my stuff, I dropped all pretense. I let my glamour fade and threw my hands out, sending a powerful jet of fire to him.

The monster howled and clambered back.

But then the others came forward.

I stood in the tight hollow trunk, my legs apart and my arms raised, and sent my fire to the monsters, maiming them as best as I could. Until the ground started shaking and a loud groaning filled the air. In seconds, the tree was ripped from its roots, and I fell forward, faceplanting on the wet ground.

One of the monsters closed its hand around my arms and torso and lifted me in the air as if I was a bug.

He said something, followed by a hoarse sound that seemed like laughter. The others followed suit.

I jerked against his hold, but nothing budged. I tried summoning my magic, but when the monster tightened his grip around me, making me dizzy and breathless, it was hard to focus. I lost the hold on my magic.

And soon, I lost the hold on my consciousness.

2

LAYLA

I PULLED the hood of my black cloak lower over my face, held on tighter to my basket, and stepped out of the trees and into the narrow path leading to the marketplace.

The marketplace was a long corridor of wooden stands, erected between a natural part of the forest, where the trees curved and created a canopy against the harsh double suns. It happened only twice a month, and brought together the many races that inhabited this realm.

Orcs, gnolls, ogres, trolls, goblins, and even a handful of fae and humans—the last two races slaves to the monsters.

Usually, when put together, all these races would be at each other's throats in seconds. But there was a silent treaty here. While everyone was trading, there would be no arguments, no fights, no bloodshed.

And most important of all: the orcs and trolls wouldn't capture innocents to eat.

I shuddered, remembering the few times I had narrowly escaped such a fate, especially when I had arrived in this forsaken land a little over five years ago and didn't know any better.

Now, even the trolls gave me a wide berth.

Well, most of them anyway.

I reached the first stands—some goblins sold trinkets they had stolen from others, orcs had custom-made swords and daggers, gnolls traded spices, and hobbits had some specialty cloaks and armor.

From under my hood, I saw as the creatures noticed my arrival. Like a blanket, a hush fell over the marketplace, but as I kept on moving, pretending I hadn't noticed anything, they resumed their activities almost as normally as before.

Without wasting my time, I went directly to one of the stands in the middle of the marketplace. Juniha, the half-hobbit, half-gnoll who tended the stand, was known for her "delicious" breads and cakes—delicious had a different meaning here. If these creatures had even tasted the food of the other three realms I had visited prior to coming here, then they would know what delicious meant.

I stopped in front of the stand, and Juniha smirked her sharp, yellow teeth at me. "I thought you wouldn't come." She stared at me with her dark eyes, her face distorted by the snout-like nose, a wide mouth, and long chin. She was stocky and short, and fur covered her thick neck and shoulders. I should be used to creatures like her by now, but sometimes I still thought I had stepped into the pages of a fantasy book— a dark and dangerous one.

"I had to deal with some pests," I answered in the common language. It had taken me awhile to learn it, and still now, I had to be extra careful with my accent.

"Again?" she asked, pretending to be interested. She

wasn't. All she wanted was to buy the herbs and spices I sold, which she used to make her breads and cakes. But since we started business years ago, she knew better than to ignore me.

"It seems it'll always be like that," I mumbled. Already tired from the trek here, and knowing I had to cross a good part of the forest to return home, I put my basket on her stand. "All right, here it is."

I unloaded all the herbs and spices, and she paid me in silver and bronze coins. As she handed me the money, she said the same thing she always did. "I wonder what you want with so much coin."

"Maybe one day I'll tell you."

She snorted, an awkward sound with her big nose, and then she looked to the side and yelled something to another gnoll in her own language.

Glad to have already been forgotten, I hooked the empty basket around my arm and turned to leave.

And froze.

The fae girl I had seen a handful of times hunkered in front of the stand across the path, her shoulders curled forward, her head low. Her auburn hair was dirtier than the last time I had seen her, and she had new purple bruises along her arms. And the damn metal shackles were still around her wrists and ankles—the four points connected to each other, to prevent her from running and getting too far if she ever decided to escape.

I clenched my jaw and held on tighter to my basket, trying to calm the rage building inside me. She was barely a child, though I knew fae aged differently than humans and witches. She could well be a hundred years old, but to her people she was probably a teenager.

And yet, somehow, she had ended up here a little over three years ago and was immediately captured by a vile troll. She had been his slave ever since. If I didn't fear ruining my disguise, and if I didn't know her captor was so nefarious, I would have freed her by now. But I knew him and he wouldn't rest until he had her back, until he made her and the other who helped her pay for bothering him.

There was nowhere I could take her.

There were no portals out of here, unfortunately.

The girl turned and her hazel eyes met mine for a brief second. Then, she recoiled deeper into herself and rushed to the next stand.

I shook my head and shooed those feelings away. There was no reason to think about escape, or leaving, or saving anyone.

Not anymore.

I forced myself to move, to walk away. I had finished my business. Now, I could go back to my cottage and pretend this world was anything other than what it truly was.

"I heard it from the ogres," a goblin told a kitsune as I walked past their stand.

"A new fae? Here?" The kitsune snorted, as if that was hard to believe. It *was* hard to believe, and for that, I stopped in my tracks and listened. "I doubt that."

"I'm telling you," the goblin said, her words slurring under the common language. "I had to go to their keep this morning to deliver some supplies. It was all the ogres talked about."

"Hm, if that's true, the fae won't last long," the kitsune added.

I sucked in a sharp breath. The kitsune was right. If the

ogres had gotten their hands on a pure-blooded fae, then the fae didn't have much time.

Which meant I also didn't have much time.

I resumed walking. Once I was out of the marketplace, I pulled the hood of my cloak away from my face and started running.

I had to get to the ogres' keep before they ate the fae.

3

I woke up in total darkness. It took my eyes a few moments before they adjusted to the dark and I could make out certain shapes—a wooden cot where I was seated, rough stone walls surrounding me, and a big metal door with an opening at the top where a little flickering light streamed in.

I shot up and instantly sat down as a wave of dizziness assaulted me. I pressed a hand over my head and felt a small egg on the back. Oh, blaze, now I remembered. The ogres ... they had gotten me. Somehow, I had hit my head, and I was now in what looked like a dungeon.

Slowly, I tried standing again and went to the door. Obviously, the cell had been designed to hold creatures much larger than me, because the cot could fit three of me, and the door was at least twice my height, its opening too far for me to even reach it.

Still disoriented and somewhat tired, I rested my back against the metal door.

What the blaze did I do now?

I couldn't stay here. I called my magic, intent on fighting my way out of this place. I turned my palms up and a tiny spark of fire flickered in my hands before dying out.

The door opened and I scurried to the other side of the cell, trying once more to call my magic in vain.

A monster filled the door. He huffed at me, said something I couldn't understand, and then pushed a jug in my direction. I clenched my fists and every cell in my body screamed for me to do something. To attack him. To blast him with my fire and run, but my fire wouldn't obey me. I couldn't even hold on to it.

A moment later, the ogre left and locked the door again.

I gritted my teeth and extended my hand in front of me, calling my fire. Again, it flickered in my palm, but faded away a second later.

A new voice rang from the door.

I looked up at the dark shape standing at the door's opening. "What did you say?"

"I don't know fae," the shape said one of the many human languages. "Can you understand me now?"

"I can," I said, in broken English. I had learned it long ago and hadn't used it in decades. "What did you mean, it won't work?"

"Your magic won't work in here because the ogres have the dungeon warded against magic."

Oh, blaze, there went my plan. Then maybe he could help me. "Who are you?"

The shape laughed, the sound muffled. "You have no idea what you've gotten yourself into."

At first, I thought all I saw was a dark silhouette because of the faint light coming from its back, but when the shape evaporated, becoming smoke and swirling in front of the opening before floating away, I shook my head.

Blazing sun, I must have hit my head harder than I thought.

A hand appeared in the opening, as if waving the smoke away.

"Ugh, I hate these liches," a new voice said. A woman. She held on to the bars of the opening, a tattoo of a star on top of her right hand, and glanced down at me. "Are you okay in there?"

"Hm, y-yes." I frowned. "What's a lich?"

"These shadow beings," she said, sounding normal. "They lurk in the shadows and prey on the weak."

That was when I realized she was speaking my language. "You're fae?"

"No, not even close." A hood covered most of her head, though I could see some of her blond curls sneaking from underneath it. "Never mind the liches. I heard the ogres captured you yesterday." She let out a long sigh. "I'm glad they haven't eaten you yet."

I gaped at her form. "Eaten me?"

"Yeah, most ogres are cannibals. Not as bad as the trolls, though." She waved her star tattoo. "Okay, tell me, do you have your medallion with you?"

I frowned. How did she know about the medallions? "Hm, if I had it with me, I wouldn't be here."

She cursed under her breath. "So you're stuck here?" she asked, though it sounded rhetorical. "Then you're of no use to me."

She let go of the bars of the opening and jumped down.

"Wait!" I called, going to the door. I rested my hands on

the metal. "Hey, come back," I shouted, suddenly fearing she was going to leave ... and leave me here. "Are you there?"

No one answered me.

Scorching sun. Something I had never felt before bloomed in my chest, and I sat down on the cold stone floor.

It was hopeless.

4

LAYLA

I COULDN'T BELIEVE I hadn't thought of it before. I had been so excited with the possibilities ... of course the fae didn't have the damn medallion. If he did, he wouldn't be here, would he? No one ended up in this land willingly. And if they did, it was only for three seconds.

I was so stupid.

Still, a foreign feeling tugged at my chest. Should I have saved him anyway? He was locked in those dungeons, all alone and probably being prepared to be served as a fresh meal to those horrible ogres. And I had left him there to die.

No, the fae was not my concern. I had too many problems as it was. I didn't need to add to the pile, especially not with a stranger.

Putting those thoughts aside, I let out a long sigh and glanced at the darkening sky as I walked back to my cottage. The two suns hovered on the horizon; one of them had already disappeared behind the trees.

I remember the first time I had seen the two suns. I had

been in awe and disbelief. The suns weren't the same size. One was much larger than the other, and more orange than yellow ... and hotter. Though this place sometimes reminded me of a muddy swamp, it was almost always too hot for my taste.

Today had not been an exception. It had been a scorching day and wearing this heavy cloak didn't help, but the "costume" helped my reputation. The reputation it had taken me a long while to build. The reputation that had kept me alive longer than I had dared hope.

I veered off the main road onto a less traveled path through the forest, one that would take me closer to my hidden cottage.

I weaved through the trees and walked the path for about fifty yards, then my steps faltered. Coming in the opposite direction was Haijen, the evil troll. His bluish skin had a permanent sick-hue, and his abnormally long limbs were strong and corded with muscles and dark veins. Thick tusks curled from his mouth up to his cheeks, almost as long as his pointed ears. He wore a thick leather skirt and a belt where a handful of crude axes hung.

Fear snaked around my bones. I'd had a run in with this troll before, long ago, when I first arrived in this cursed land. Lost, I ended up in his hideout, or whatever he called that corner where he lived. I didn't know it was his land, I didn't know anything about trolls, and I surely didn't know they were greedy, possessive, deadly predators.

The troll had attacked me and I barely escaped intact. As I fled, he promised that the next time I crossed his path, he would put me out of my misery.

I believed him.

And he was true to his word. I had encountered him a

couple of times before and he had immediately charged me. I had run from him until he gave up the chase.

So, this time, before he saw me, I hopped off the path and hid behind a tree. I even slowed my breathing and put a magic blanket over me, so he wouldn't hear or smell me.

His footsteps grew louder and soon I heard more. The sounds of metal clanking together. I couldn't help myself and spied around the tree.

The fear I felt was only eclipsed by the protectiveness that surged up inside me at the sight of his slave trudging along behind him, the chains around her wrists and ankles bruising her fair skin.

The young female fae from the marketplace.

Her head was low and her shoulders sagged, as if she had already given up living, but wasn't allowed to die.

If only I could save her …

If only I could protect her …

But I could barely protect myself, and I certainly wasn't saved. I was just surviving.

I stayed crouched behind the tree as the troll and his slave walked past me on the path, going back to his hideout, for sure.

And I stayed there for a long time, feeling like the worst coward of this realm and all of the other realms.

5

I KNEW I WAS DREAMING, but it didn't really feel like a dream.

I stood in front of one of the large windows at the Summer Palace, the Sun City shining bright behind the inner walls under the scorching sun.

My favorite place in the entire Wyth. My home.

I turned around and found myself staring at a low and wide beige bed, the soft yellow covers ruffled and folded at the foot of the bed. And on the other side, propped by many golden pillows, was my mother.

My heart stopped.

My mother's hair, usually tight into a neat bun at the nape of her neck, was long and loose, like a black curtain around her shoulders. Her dark skin was ashen, her hazel eyes dull and sunken, and her lips were parched.

She looked sick.

Had Sanna's magic hurt her so badly that she still hadn't healed?

"Mother," I called her, walking to her bedside.

But she didn't look at me, she didn't acknowledge me.

Instead, she inhaled a deep breath and rasped, "Henia."

The double doors at the other side opened, but instead of my mother's handmaiden, Mahaeru entered, one of the Wyth goddesses.

Her long, black hair flowed behind her as if a nonexistent breeze whipped it back as she strode toward my mother's bed.

My mother's back straightened. "Mahaeru, what are you doing here?"

The goddess halted at the foot of my mother's bed. "Queen Natsia, I'm here to check on you." The goddess's eyes scanned my mother's body. "How are you managing the poison today?"

I gaped at them. "Poison? What the blaze?"

"The same." My mother lay back on the pillows. "It's slowly spreading, taking me inch by inch."

"And the medicine I brought yesterday?"

"Helps with the pain," my mother said. "And a little with my energy. But nothing can stop the poison. We've called all the healers from Wyth, and they all said the same. A magic poison can only be—"

"Cured by the witch who spelled it, or another equally powerful witch." The goddess gave one short nod. "With Sanna dead, we can't find any other. Either there's no other witch in Wyth, or they all went into hiding."

"Which means it won't take long for the poison to take me."

"But we can delay it." The goddess pointed to the glass on the bedside table. "Keep drinking the medicine and it should delay the poison."

"Delay it, not stop it." My mother sighed. "It's fine. I just have to last until we find my son." She was looking for me? I mean, I knew she probably would, but with this poison—something that I was having trouble getting my head around—she should be focusing on her health, not on me. *"I've sent my most trusted*

soldiers into countless realms after Varian, but no one has found him yet."

The goddess, who always seemed stoic and sometimes harsh, let out a long breath. "I've been trying too, but I can't find him either."

My mother's hands clenched around the blanket covering her legs. "We need to find him, Mahaeru. If we don't, there will be no heir to take my place when I'm gone. And I'm afraid I'll be going sooner than all of us thought."

No, no, no. What in the scorching heat was she talking about? I pressed a hand to my forehead. This was too much. Magic poison? Dying? Heir?

"Queen Natsia, there's more," Mahaeru started, her voice as solemn as always. "Because of the uncertainty of the future of the Summer Court, unrest has been plaguing the people, and the fae are taking advantage of that."

My mother frowned. "What do you mean?"

"A few southern village magistrates are banding together and trying to create a more organized rebel group. If Prince Varian isn't back by the time you die, they plan on seizing the throne."

What?

My mother paled more. "No," she whispered. "My kingdom will fall into chaos. The peace and prosperity my family spent decades building will be undone."

"Civil war will certainly start without Varian," Mahaeru added.

"We cannot allow that." My mother pressed a hand to her chest. "Mahaeru, if you can, please, call General Behar for me. We need to stop this mess from taking shape if we can."

"Agreed." Mahaeru nodded. She whipped her head in my direction and her eyes met mine. "Meanwhile, we can only hope Prince Varian finds his away back quickly."

With a gasp, I sat up on the cot. I was drenched in sweat, my heartbeat fast, and my breathing came in shallow gasps.

I knew it hadn't been just a dream. I had been a vision, an image of a moment that Mahaeru had been able to send to me while I slept.

I rubbed at my chest, my mind swirling with so much information.

My mother had been poisoned; Sanna had been killed. Now, an uprising was threatening to divide my kingdom. I shook my head. There was so much in the dark still ... how had the fight ended? If Vasant had won and kept the Spring Court for himself, Mahaeru would have found a way to let me know. Because, if that had happened, I was sure Vasant would have turned toward the Summer Court first and immediately launched an attack. Hopefully, Hayley and Ash were now queen and king and at least that problem was resolved.

I glanced around the cold walls of my dungeon cell, as if one would suddenly melt away and I would be able to run away from here.

Sadly, I didn't have that kind of magic.

Heavy footsteps echoed in the hallway and I stood on top of my cot, but even like that I still couldn't see much from the door's top opening. A few seconds later, one ugly ogre stopped in front of my door and opened it. Even knowing my magic wouldn't work in here, I called it. Better to have a few sparks to fight with than nothing at all.

Three more ogres appeared behind the first one and my shoulders sagged. Maybe I could fight hand to hand against one of them, but four? If only I had my sword with me.

The first creature yelled something at me in their foreign tongue. When I didn't move, he and another ogre stepped into my cell and came for me. I took a few steps back and analyzed my chances. They reached for me, and I jumped out of the way. I sprang onto the hard cot and made for the door.

Three ogres blocked the doorway, but I wouldn't give up now.

But before I could do anything, huge hands closed around my shoulders and arms.

"Hey!" I jerked against the monsters' grip.

They ignored me and dragged me from the cell. I thrashed against their hold, but their grip tightened until my body ached. I stopped fighting.

For now.

Despite it all, I tried paying attention to where they were taking me, and more importantly to the hallways, doors, and windows we walked by. There wasn't much to this place. We left the dungeon, which was underground as I suspected, and emerged into a long corridor of gray stone, but a little smoother and lighter than the ones below. The space was wider too and better illuminated with sconces of shimmering torchlight every few feet. I spotted long horizontal openings in the wall, like windows, some with rough curtains, but most with nothing to cover it. Beyond the windows, the two suns were hidden behind clouds, though it didn't look like it would rain. It was hard to tell what time of day it was.

The ogres dragged me across a wide room and then under an archway that opened to a round room. In the center was a fur rug—I didn't want to know the animal it had belonged to—and around it were several wooden chairs.

Three of the chairs were occupied: two ogres and someone else.

A woman with short brown hair and pale skin sat between the monsters. She looked small in the large chair, but she held her back straight like an arrow and her pointed chin high. She wore a brown gown that had seemed put together from several rags and a necklace of long tusks.

I was pushed to the ground and fell on all fours in front of the chairs. A sudden ray of light blinded me, and I realized a circular window high on the wall, close to the ceiling. I tried raising my hands to cover the peeking sun from my face, but the chains around my wrists were too tight.

Without losing her composure, the woman hopped down from her chair and walked closer. Her brown eyes never faltered from my gaze as she walked circled me.

I wanted to ask her who she was, what she was doing here, why she was mixed up with these monsters, but she didn't look fae—she had no pointed ears—and she probably didn't speak my language anyway.

She stopped in front of me. "Strong, aren't you?"

I gaped at her. She was speaking my language. "I—"

"He'll do," she said in English to one of the ogres. "It'll take a couple of days. Just make sure he's not hurt until then."

"Wait." I pushed up to my feet and took a couple of steps toward her. "What's going on? Who are you?"

The ogres' hands closed around my shoulders and pulled me back.

"Don't bother with silly questions, fae," she said, looking at me from the corner of her eyes as if she was disgusted with me. She had gone back to fae language. "Just be a good boy and rest in your cell. It'll all end soon."

"End? What do you mean?"

One corner of her lips tugged up. "It's none of your business." She waved her hand at me. "You can take him back now," she said in English.

The ogres tugged me back. "Wait! Wait!" I jerked against their holds, but they were too strong for me.

"Ah, and don't forget to give him a bath," the woman said matter-of-factly. "He stinks." She then turned to the other two ogres in the chairs. "I heard you had trouble with the Bloodwrath witch again."

"Bloodwrath didn't do anything, but she was spotted a few days ago," one of the ogres said, his voice deep and rough and the words slurred and unsure. It was gritting on my nerves to see them all speaking a human language, but that only made me assume this woman was human.

"So what's the matter?" the woman asked.

"She's a witch!" the one ogre said. "She's powerful. She has done too much to us already. We want her gone."

The woman examined her nails. "She's powerful, yes, but she has been quiet lately. I don't think there's a necessity to go after her and kill her."

One of the ogres leaned forward. "Are you afraid of her, Carlyn?"

The woman balked. "Of course not!" Even from across the room, I could see her cheeks growing red.

I let the ogres take me, my mind reeling with this new piece of information. I had no idea who Carlyn was, but if she was in league with these ogres, it meant she was powerful, and if she was powerful but was afraid of the Bloodwrath, then it meant this witch was even more powerful. They were all afraid of her.

Perhaps I was deluding myself, but if there was a powerful witch out there, I had to find her. She could be my ticket home.

I had to come up with a solid plan to escape.

I WAITED in my cell patiently. First, the ogres brought me food —something that looked like porridge but smelled and tasted nothing like it. I forced myself to eat it because I needed to keep my strength up.

Second, I knew the creatures would take me out of my cell at some point because that Carlyn woman had told them to give me a bath. So, when they finally came for me the next day, I pretended to fight back, as if I didn't want to be taken from my cell, as if I was afraid they would kill me. I was careful not to say anything since it seemed some of these ogres could speak more than one or two languages.

I was dragged out of the dungeon, led to another part of the building, and finally pushed into what looked like a private courtyard. I blinked several times, trying to adjust my eyes to the sudden brightness of the two suns. From the way they shone down on me, I could tell it was early in the day, but soon they would heat up, and the air would be as blistering as the desert in the Summer Court.

I forced myself to open my eyes and take stock of my surroundings. Brownish grass, high concrete walls, and a few yards away, a wooden building.

The ogres took me inside; it was an outhouse. One side had a large wooden tub, and the other side held what looked like stalls and holes on the ground for toilets.

The smell inside this outhouse was unbearable, but at least the water in the tub looked clean.

Not that I would have time to find out.

Once the two ogres and I were alone in the outhouse, I called my fire. Glad to know this part of their keep wasn't warded, I let the fire engulf my arms and sent potent blasts toward the monsters. They shrieked and jerked back, letting go of me so they wouldn't be burned.

I didn't waste time.

I jumped and conjured fire jets underneath my feet, which gave me enough propulsion to arch over the tub and land on the other side of the outhouse, where there was another door.

I ran out and didn't stop running, not even when I faced the wall. I used the fire jet under my feet again to jump over the wall. When I landed on the other side, I found myself at the edge of a forest.

Blaze. I would probably get lost in here, but it was better than staying and getting caught again. The angry shouts of the ogres bellowed from the other side of the fortress wall.

I placed a glamour over myself and ran into the forest, determined to find Bloodwrath.

6

LAYLA

THE DAMNED IMPS had played in my garden again. Those little demons. I didn't really know what they were, what they were called—like most of the creatures from this realm. Besides the ogres and trolls and goblins and a couple more, I didn't know what the dozens of different monsters I had encountered were. I just gave them a name so I could call them something in my head.

Sometimes I wondered how many different monsters were in this world that I hadn't met yet. I shuddered, hoping I never would. The ones I already knew were more than enough.

I grabbed my rake and started piling the herbs they had pulled out from their beds and spread through the grass. The little imps often came out at night—and sometimes during the day too, like today—and just made a mess. They were naughty and reminded me of children with too much energy. They never attacked me directly unless I attacked them first. Then, they were nasty. I just wanted them to leave me alone!

But they were the only ones who didn't seem to care about my reputation.

I piled the herbs carefully, hoping I could salvage some and sell them at the marketplace next month, but something else caught my attention. A thin line of upturned earth, going from the back of the garden into the woods.

"Oh, no, not again," I muttered. I dropped the rake and followed the line through the thin trees, a few yards into the forest, until it reached a small clearing, shadowed by the trees' crowns, but still well illuminated by sunlight.

The line stopped at the wood plaque I had made and staked to the ground. The mound of earth in front of it was intact this time, at least. I ran my hand over the ground, smoothing the earth. I swear when I saw these imps again, I would skin them alive.

A twig snapped and some ruffling came from the cottage.

Oh, those little imps would meet their fate right now.

I opened myself to my magic and went to meet them.

7

I RAN without rest and without direction for hours. All that mattered was to get away from those monsters, far enough away they wouldn't be able to catch up with me.

Weary with fatigue, I allowed myself to rest.

I didn't drop my glamour, though, because I could hear and sense other creatures close by and the last thing I needed was another fight, another scuffle that would send me back to square one.

After some rest, I looked for someone to help me out. I was probably delusional, feverish and whatnot, but I had seen Carlyn inside the ogres' lair. If there was a woman like her—not a monster who was willing to bite my head off at first sight—in that fortress, there was bound to be someone else on the outside too.

It took me a while and many narrow encounters with different creatures, but I found a row of precarious market stalls in a wide clearing in the forest.

I was trying to develop a plan of how I would sneak into what seemed a marketplace and ask in my language about

Bloodwrath, when a short and stocky monster walked out of the stand row and into the forest.

With greenish skin, long nails, and a huge, round nose, the creature looked like it could give me a good fight, but I didn't give it a chance. The moment it walked by a tree a few yards into the forest, I wrapped my fire around it, immobilizing it.

"Do you speak my language?" I asked, my voice rough. I leaned over the creature, fire-like daggers coming out of my hands, and pointed the weapons at its face. "Answer me."

The creature mumbled in a different tongue.

Blaze. "Can you understand me now?" I said, changing to English.

"Y-yes, a little," the creature stuttered. I let out a relieved sigh. It would have been messy if I had to let him go and grab someone else. "What do you want?"

"Where can I find Bloodwrath?"

The creature's glassy gray eyes went wide. "She's dangerous. You should not go to her."

I tightened my fire around him, still not burning, but warm enough to give him a fright, and brought the fire in my hand closer to his face. "Answer me! Where can I find this witch?"

"I d-do not know! Nobody knows! But I hear she is often seen in the woods." The creature pointed his hand to the other end of the marketplace. "That way. That's what I know."

I frowned. He could be lying. Someone else might know more than he did, but I didn't have time or the will to let him go so he could warn others of my presence, or to grab another monster for more information.

I marched in the direction the creature told me.

When I was a quarter of a mile away, I let my magic drop and the creature go.

I SEARCHED for hours without luck. At some point, I was sure I had never been more lost in these forsaken woods. I had even come across my old hiding trunk, which was fortunate because I was able to grab the sack with my things from it—something I had thought lost by now.

Despite moving and walking all day, I hadn't found the witch. Night came and I hopped into a tree, staying high on one of its branches, glamoured to all. Every sound and little movement put me on high alert, but thankfully no creature saw me or attacked me. I was sure the ogres would come after me. They would find me when I was sleeping, and I wouldn't have time to wake up and fight properly.

But thankfully, that didn't happen.

In the morning, right before the two suns rose, I resumed my trek.

After a couple of hours, sweating and hungry, I was convinced I had either misunderstood about this Bloodwrath witch and she didn't even exist, or I had been tricked and was on the wrong path—the latter was a good possibility. Why the blaze would a strange creature help me when I was threatening him?

I didn't know how long had passed. My legs were trembling, tired. My stomach growled, hungry as it had never been. My eyes wanted to close, take a break. But I kept pushing. I had to find this witch. She was my only hope, and I wouldn't stop searching for her until I found her.

The two suns had started their slow descent when I stumbled past a few trees and came to a thick hedge of thorns. I halted and stared at it. This didn't look natural. Someone had done this.

Perhaps a witch who wanted to be left alone.

I called my fire and took a step forward, then stopped again. What if this witch was truly fearsome and horrible as Carlyn and the ogres had made her out to be? What if she didn't hear me out? What if I was walking into a death trap?

My only hope was to be careful and do my best to get on her good side, if she had one.

I inhaled deeply and used my fire to cut a small gap in the thorn hedges, big enough for me to crawl through. The moment I crossed the hedge, they closed behind me.

Magical.

Now I was sure this was where Bloodwrath was hiding. It had to be.

With my magic under my fingertips, in case I had to defend myself, I slowly advanced. The trees here were tall and thin, and they became scarce the more I moved forward until they finally opened up into a wide garden and small wooden cottage.

I frowned, taking everything in. The garden was immaculate, with a variety of plants and colorful flowerbeds. A dark wooden bench separated the garden from a long patch of diverse herbs. Some I had never seen before, all of them bright green and strong. The cottage looked old but quaint and well taken care of. There was a small table and a rocking chair on the porch and a neatly folded blanket over it.

Whoever lived here couldn't be an evil witch.

Could she?

I made my way to the porch, still holding my magic. I

raised my fist to knock on the door, but sensed movement behind me.

I turned fast and saw someone at the edge of the forest across the garden. A woman. A beautiful woman with long blond curls, striking blue eyes, and fair and smooth skin.

This couldn't be Bloodwrath.

She drew a small, crude dagger from the pocket of her blue dress and pointed it at me. "What are you doing here?"

I stared at her. Something about her was familiar. She took a step forward, her curls bouncing around her shoulders. She turned the dagger in her grip and I saw the star tattoo covering her hand. "Answer me!"

Scorching sun, I knew where I had met this woman before. "It's you," I rasped.

8

LAYLA

WHAT THE HELL was that fae doing here? I didn't need a dagger, but I wanted to look fierce to him without resorting to my magic. The fewer people who knew what I could do, the better.

Still, how had he escaped? How had he found me? And why?

"You're the woman who came to my cell and asked about the medallion," the fae said, his voice deep. He looked like a homeless man I had seen before in the human world—with his brown hair like a nest of snakes on his back, dirt on his face and hands, and his clothes in rags and grimy. Even his boots were covered in mud. "Why did you leave me there?"

I shrugged. "You didn't have what I wanted."

"And that's reason enough to leave an innocent to be devoured by those monsters?"

"I don't know you, so I don't really care what happens to you."

He took a step closer and I took a step back, raising the dagger a little more. "What the hell are you doing?"

He rolled his shoulders and let out a long breath, as if trying to calm himself down. "Are you the Bloodwrath witch?"

"No," I said too fast.

"You are!" He seemed content about that. "You ... I thought you would be an old hag with a wart on your nose or a hunchback."

I rolled my eyes. "How many fairy tale books have you read?"

"Not many," he said. "I was busy reading books about politics and fae magic."

"All right, enough of this shit." I brandished the dagger in his direction. "What are you doing *here*?"

"I heard how powerful and scary you are. The scary part is still up for debate, but I'm hoping you're powerful."

I raised an eyebrow. "And why is that?"

"So you can take me home."

He didn't have the medallion, but he wanted to go back to his realm. Welcome to the club! "I'll give you a similar answer to the one you gave me a couple of days ago: If I could use my magic to take someone to another realm, I wouldn't be here."

His wide shoulders deflated. "But ..."

Suddenly, the fae looked like a lost puppy, one that could still bite my fingers off, I was sure, but something tugged inside my chest. Five years ago, I had just arrived here alone. I had wandered this land, praying I would live another day, another hour. I hid from monsters and became scared of every shadow, every click.

I wished there had been someone who had been kind to me, helped me figure out a few things, even if in the end I still had to go on my own way and be alone.

I let out a long sigh and lowered my dagger.

"Stay here," I told him as I walked past him, giving him a wide berth, and went inside my cottage.

It was small, with a living room, a kitchen with only a table and a wall on the side, and one bedroom. The bathroom was outside and there was no shower.

I went into my bedroom and rummaged through the trunk I had there—a trunk I had found in another abandoned cottage miles from here. Most of my furniture and belongings had come from other houses and villages, places that had been abandoned who knew why or how.

I found a large tunic, grabbed a clean cloth, and in the kitchen, I found an unused bar of soap I had made a few weeks ago. I hugged everything and went back outside.

The fae was still standing in the same spot, though now he had his arms crossed and a knot adorned his forehead. He glanced at me, suspicious. "What is that?"

"A cloth for a towel, soap, and shirt I hope fits." I handed them to him. He took it and I instantly backed away several steps. "There's a small lake a hundred yards or so that way." I pointed to the line of trees behind him. "The water is usually warm."

He stared at the things I had given him for a moment, then brought his eyes back to me. Only then I saw his eyes were a luminous dark golden-green color. "Thanks."

I nodded and watched as he turned around and disappeared into the forest.

WHILE THE FAE WAS GONE, I made a creamy vegetable and herb soup, grabbed some blankets from the trunk in my bedroom, and left them on the couch in the living room. The couch was made of wood and leather, not too comfortable, and I started to think the tall fae wouldn't fit on it. But that was up to him. If he wanted to sleep on the floor, he could. As long as he stayed far from me.

I was starting to think the fae had been found by a wild kitsune and eaten, when almost an hour later, I heard his heavy footsteps on the porch. He knocked on the closed door.

"Come in," I said, feeling weird. Why the hell was I helping this fae again? I didn't owe anything to anyone. I had been alone in this realm for many years. Certainly, I didn't need anyone.

The door opened and the fae stepped in.

I stared at him, confused. This couldn't be the same fae I had sent to the lake. He looked completely different. He looked handsome. His face was devoid of dirt, and for the first time I could see the sharp edges of his jaw and chin. His olive skin was smooth and unblemished, and his long brown hair, now damp and clean, fell behind his back. He was as tall, but the tunic I had given him hugged his entire torso. I realized he also had a wide set of shoulders, and his arms, corded with muscles, barely fit in the sleeves.

He had his pants back on, though I could see they were damp too, which meant he had washed them in the lake. Even his hips and thighs were strong. From the little I had seen, I could tell he was pure muscle and strength and—

I shook my head, ridding myself of those thoughts.

Yes, he was handsome and hot, but I had more important things to worry about.

I pointed to the kitchen. "There's also soup on the wood stove." Next, I gestured to the blankets on the couch. "You can sleep here." I glanced back at him, sure he wouldn't fit on the couch. That was his problem.

I turned toward my bedroom.

"Wait, I—"

"You should rest," I said, my back to him. I didn't know why, but for some reason, I needed a minute or two to myself. "We can talk in the morning."

I entered my room, closed and locked the door, and just to be sure, I called my magic and put a ward around the door and windows. If he tried to come into my room to kill me, I would know.

Then, I retreated to my bed and wondered once more what the hell I was doing.

9

VARIAN

Mahaeru stood behind the closed doors of my mother's room, General Behar in front of her.

"What is the latest news?" she asked, serious and somber as usual.

"It's true," Behar said. "A few leaders in the south have joined forces and they are building an army. Their excuse is that if the queen dies and the prince isn't found, they will need the means to keep their towns and villages safe." He shook his head. "But I've sent a spy in their midst. It seems what they are planning is to lay claim to the throne."

Mahaeru tsked. "Things are heating up fast."

Behar nodded. "They certainly are. I sent an order to have a squadron posted on the main roads leading to Sun City. Hopefully, that will discourage anyone from attacking."

"I'm not sure that will be enough," said the goddess.

Behar glanced at the closed door beside them. "How is she?"

"The pain is sharper today," Mahaeru said. "She's trying to disguise it, but it drains her energy. She has been in and out of sleep all day." She turned to the window at the end of the corridor,

the sky orange from the sunset. "I'll bring her more medicine soon."
Her eyes turned to me and she looked directly at me. "I'll do all I
can until Prince Varian finds his way back."

I sat up on the floor, the blanket knotted around my legs, and inhaled deeply.

The way Mahaeru looked at me in the dreams ... they couldn't be just dreams, could they? Deep down, I knew they weren't dreams. I had already come to terms with that. The way she talked about me coming back bothered me, as if it was a done deal, as if all I had to do was snap my fingers and done! I would suddenly be back at the Summer Court.

I lay back down and stared at the ceiling in the near dark. Only a sliver of moonlight came in from the closed windows, and the occasional gust of wind rustled the leaves outside.

Other than that, the cottage was quiet.

I glanced at the closed door, which the witch had disappeared through hours ago. She had offered me a bath in a way I hadn't had in weeks, delicious food—anything was better than the odd things I had been eating out in the wild—and a place to sleep. The couch had proven too small for me, and too weak. I was afraid that if I let my full weight on it, it would break. So, I spread one of the blankets she gave me over the beaten up leather rug in front of the couch and slept there.

Slept was a polite word for what I was doing. I felt too restless and anxious, and each time I closed my eyes, I had dreams of my mother or Mahaeru. Or both.

My muscles ached to move, but I didn't give in. It was still the middle of the night. I had to be quiet and try to sleep. If I had strange dreams again, so be it.

And if those weren't dreams, then they were telling me something I already knew: my kingdom and I were doomed.

I DIDN'T SLEEP AS MUCH as I hoped. Early morning, I was up and ready to do something. I found some bread in the kitchen and ate that for breakfast, and then went outside.

It didn't take long for me to find something to do: in a corner of the garden was a stump of a tree and a crude ax. Beside them were logs ready to be cut. Hoping I wouldn't wake up the witch, I started working.

I focused on the task, cutting the firewood fast and efficiently, and worked my arms and shoulders and back. It was a good break for my busy mind.

The two suns had already peeked from behind the trees when the witch emerged from the cottage, and I took a good look at her.

Yesterday, I had noticed she was too pretty, but in the sunlight, my breath caught.

Her blond curls adorned her shoulders, shining under the sun. Fair skin stretched over delicate features—small nose, thin brows, and rose lips. And her eyes ... her eyes shone like two huge sapphires. Today, she wore a simple green dress exposing the soft swell of her breasts and emphasizing her tiny waist.

She didn't look like a monster from this realm, or even a powerful witch.

She looked like an angel.

I lowered the ax. "Did I wake you?"

She shook her head, her curls bouncing side to side. "You don't need to do that."

"I know."

Her brows curled down as she watched me for a moment. "Who are you? How did you end up here?"

I rested the ax beside the tree stump and took a few steps closer to her. She went rigid, but didn't move away. "I'm Prince Varian of the Summer Court." Her bright eyes widened. "I crossed a witch's portal by mistake." I bet she was wondering how someone crossed a witch's portal by mistake. I wouldn't tell her that. Not yet, at least. "How about you?"

She didn't answer right away, and for a moment, I thought she wouldn't. "My name is Layla." I waited to see if she would tell me how she got here, but she didn't, and I didn't push it. "So what's your plan?"

I stood tall in front of her, hoping my princely manners shone through the rags I was wearing and the situation I was in. "I want your help. There must be a way for me to go back to the fae realm."

Layla shook her head. "No—"

"If you help me," I interrupted her, "if you find a way to get me home, you can come with me. I'll give you riches; I'll pay you whatever you want." I was getting desperate here, but at this point, I would do anything. "I'll even give you a medallion so you can use it to go to any realm you want."

Her eyes shone clearer as she stared at me in visible shock.

Now I had her.

10

LAYLA

Prince Varian's offer was tempting. For a brief moment, I let myself dream about it. About leaving this place, about receiving a bag full of gold and a medallion, and going back to the witches' realm.

But that was impossible.

"Look, Prince Varian," I started. "Even if I agreed to help you, it's no good. I have already searched this forsaken land for a way out and there's none. We're stuck here."

His wide shoulders sagged down as he accepted defeat. "It can't be."

I let out a sigh. Long ago, I had been in denial too. It took me many years to understand, and accept, that I wasn't leaving this place. If I had accepted it sooner, it would have saved me a lot of trouble and pain.

"Just ... you should head north, toward the coast," I told him. It was a plan of mine, but I had never gone that way. "I hear that even though the way there is riddled with monsters, the coast is better. Fewer monsters. You should be able to settle there."

The big fae shook his head. "No, it can't be."

I wanted to shoo him away. The sooner he left, the better it would be for me. Less mess, less complication, less attachment. The last thing I needed was to get involved with a fae in this forsaken land and make things even worse for myself.

But at the same time, I didn't have the heart to send him away when he looked like a lost puppy. I had been there, suffered and cried and raged. I had gone through all that alone.

My reputation as Bloodwrath was quite fierce and made me look like a heartless, bloody old crone, but despite all the losses and heartaches I had lived through, I wasn't. Not really.

"Look," I started again. "You—" Little clicks came from behind the trees. "Oh, no," I whispered.

"What—?" Varian asked, but the rest of his question was swallowed up when the little imps jumped out from the forest and invaded my garden.

The nasty bluish creatures with long and pointy ears, huge, oval dark eyes, and many, many rows of sharp teeth shrieked and jumped up and down, not one bit afraid of us. If they weren't as tall as my mid-thigh, I would be the one afraid of them.

"Be gone, little pests." I extended my arm and threw some black magic sparks at them. That only made them more upset and they started for my herb patch. "Oh no!" I brought up a thin black veil around the patch, but I knew that wouldn't hold them back long enough. I had tried that before.

Suddenly, flames appeared between the imps and the patch, a wall of fire thick and wide. I dropped my hand and stared as Prince Varian commanded the fire to advance on the imps, closing in on them and pushing them back into the forest.

The creatures yelled and jumped, trying to get away from the fire, but they couldn't without getting burned. The odd thing was, the ground where the fire had licked wasn't scorched at all.

The fire invaded the forest, pushing the imps farther and farther away.

When we couldn't see or hear the imps anymore, Prince Varian dropped his hands and turned to me. "They seem to be gone." His brows knotted. "What were those?"

"I don't know," I said, my voice low. "I just call them little imps." I pointed to the grass around us. The trees and bushes weren't burned either. "How did you do that? How was the fire burning them, but it didn't burn anything else?"

"I can control where and how my fire burns," he said simply.

Incredible.

Perhaps he could be useful. By keeping the little imps away. I was sure they would try coming again, as they usually did, but if Varian used his fire to push them out a handful of times, they would eventually give up and leave me alone.

"You can stay," I said, feeling awkward about this. "Until we figure out something for you. Like a place for you to go, or to stay, or ... something."

The fae looked at me with gentle eyes, seeming relieved by my decision.

I felt the weight of his gaze, of the small curl of his lips, of the size of his arms as he crossed them over his chest.

My cheeks started burning, and without knowing what to do, I turned around and stomped into the cottage.

11

I SNATCHED a few pieces of firewood and followed Layla inside the cottage. She went to the wood stove, where she placed a kettle of water. I approached her carefully and rested the firewood on the pile beside the stove.

I took several steps back and asked, "How do you know fae?"

Layla glanced at me from over her shoulder. "I was given the sight and the speech long ago."

I frowned, wanting to ask how and why, but the way her back straightened and her shoulders squared, I knew I shouldn't prod much. At least, not yet. Instead, I asked, "Is there anything else I can help you with?"

"Not really. Besides managing the little imps, who I think won't come back *so* soon, there's nothing much to do."

My frown deepened. If there was nothing to do, then I could think. I had to come up with a plan on how to get out of here. Even if Layla didn't believe there was a way out, I wasn't ready to give up. Especially now that I had found her. She didn't look happy about me being here, but I was relieved I wasn't alone anymore.

And according to what I had heard, she was a powerful witch. With my magic, hers, and maybe something else. Someone else? I just couldn't sit here and wait for time to pass, as if a solution or a portal would show up in front of my face.

"When I was coming this way, I saw some stands along a narrow path in the middle of the forest," I said. "Looked like a marketplace."

Nodding, Layla reached for two mugs inside a wooden cupboard. "It is a marketplace. Several races meet there to trade for a handful of days every few weeks. It's supposed to be a peaceful place, where even mortal enemies can't attack." She snorted. "But the tension there is always high and everyone expects a fight to break out."

"What do they sell there?"

She placed some herbs inside the mugs. "Everything you can imagine. Clothing, jewelry, food, herbs and spices, *magical* potions." She emphasized the word magical as if she knew they were a trick. "Sometimes there are stands for furniture, lands, and even livestock. And if you look close enough, you might be able to buy information, or even find a human or two." She shuddered.

"Humans are sold like cattle?"

Layla picked up the kettle and poured hot water into the mugs. "Well, other than the peace in the marketplace, there are no rules in this land, none I've learned of anyway." She offered one of the mugs to me. "If the ogres or the trolls want to take a goblin or pixie or a human and make him a slave, they just do it."

That was interesting, and quite disturbing. I took the mug

from her, the warmth seeping into my palms. "There are no leaders in this land? No kingdoms?"

She shook her head and held her mug. "Again, none that I know of. I've seen different ogre clans, troll villages, and things like that, but each one is independent and has their own leader. They claim a piece of the land and that's it. There's no order, no hierarchy, no border, nothing."

"Hm." I sipped from the tea and found it sweet and tasty. I drank a little more, even though it was burning my tongue. "I haven't eaten and drunk anything like this for weeks. Thanks."

"How long have you been here?"

"Three weeks, give or take a couple of days. I was really lost during my first few days," I confessed.

She nodded. "I know the feeling."

She brought her mug to her lips, her bright blue eyes fixed on mine, and I felt an urge to make her talk more, to ask her about her life. How had she come to this place? Why hadn't she tried going back? Why was she refusing to help me? Even if she said she had tried everything, she had been alone. Now she had me. She could use me, use my help. Things would be different now.

But before I brought up any crazy ideas, I needed to have a solid plan.

And for that, I had to move.

AFTER THE TEA and a few cookies that tasted like cinnamon, though Layla assured me they were made of something else entirely, she went to her garden to work. More specifically to her herb patch. As she exited the cottage, she briefly told me she sold the herbs at the marketplace.

I wanted to ask her what she did with her money, but again I locked my tongue inside my mouth. I didn't want her to kick me out of here because I was too nosy.

I stayed quiet, and when she wasn't looking, I grabbed one of the few cloaks she had hanging behind the door, sneaked out, and headed to the marketplace—wearing a glamour, of course.

LAYLA

PRINCE VARIAN of the Summer Court ...

Until now I hadn't allowed my thoughts to travel that way, but now that I was alone in the garden, with my gown's skirt hiked up and my knees pressed to the damp soil, I couldn't escape the prison of my mind.

I had heard of him before, of course. I had even seen him from afar many years ago, but back then nothing about him had struck me. That was because I had no interest in the Summer Court.

My life, my future, had been tied to the Spring Court.

I was glad I escaped that fate, but I wasn't sure I was living a better one.

My friends certainly weren't.

I shook my head and busied myself with my herbs. I checked on them, snatched the ones that looked like were dying, planted a few more, and after all was done, I pressed my fingers to the soil and sent my magic out.

Witches' powers varied greatly. Some could only do one thing, like move objects or create potions or heal, and others could do two or more things. My mentor was a witch who could do everything. She was powerful beyond compare. Sometimes I wondered what had happened to her.

As for me, I fell somewhere in between. I could do a handful of things, like helping plants grown strong and bigger than they usually would. To be honest, I didn't even know what I could do anymore. I hadn't used my full powers in years. I only used them now to work in my garden and to keep the little imps away. The showdown I performed that brought on my great evil and powerful reputation had been just that ... a show. I had used my magic to make me seem bigger and badder than I was, and it had worked.

Trolls, ogres, and other creatures of this damn land stayed away from me now, if not from outright fear, then out of respect.

And that was enough for me.

I glanced at the cottage.

Would it be enough for the summer prince?

I let out a long, dreadful sigh. What the hell was I going to do with him? I couldn't keep him here, but I also didn't have it in me to send him away. He wouldn't last a day out there by himself.

Well, he had been here for a few weeks now, and I had made it by myself, so maybe—

I shook my head again. No, my reputation might paint me as a bad guy, but I wasn't one. I couldn't in good conscience sent the prince away. I didn't like it, but he would have to stay here until we figured out something better. Perhaps if we explored the area carefully, we would find another cottage we could renovate. He could create a reputation for himself and then the monsters would keep their distance from him too and—

A growl echoed through the garden. Instantly, I shot to my feet, spilling the bowl that had been resting by my side, and called my magic.

Ogres marched toward me from the backside of the cottage, their big feet squashing the plants in my garden.

I stared in shock. They had never come close to my place, much less walked right in.

"Where's the fae?" one of them asked in their language, his big axe tight in his hand.

I frowned. "What are you talking about?"

"The fae," the ogre snapped. "We can smell him all over this place. All over you."

Varian had escaped from their dungeon and come directly here. The ogres had followed him. What did the ogres want with him, other than a nice meal? I mean, fae probably tasted better than goblins, but still, they could have anything. Why chase a fae?

"I don't know what you're talking about." I raised my hands, white bolts hovering over my palms. "Now get out before I make you."

The ogre let out a hoarse chuckle. "You might be powerful, witch, but we want the fae." He advanced on me. "You're coming with us."

No way in hell!

I threw the bolts at him, but the other ogres rushed me. My heart sped as I raised a shield around me, but the ogres clanked their weapons on it. They swiped wide and hit the wooden bench, breaking it in half. The loud crack startled me and my shield flickered. The next hit broke the shield, and before I could throw more of my magic at them, two held down my arms and tied thick ropes around my torso and arms.

"Let me go!" I screamed, jerking against the ropes.

They pressed one of their anti-magic charms on my arms. Numbness filled me and I couldn't feel my magic anymore. I screamed again, out of frustration. Desperation.

But there was nothing I could do.

They had found me unprepared, stunned with their boldness.

And now they were taking me away.

13

I DIDN'T FIND the marketplace right away. It took me a few turns and a couple of hours, and I even thought that maybe it had already been dismantled for the week. Layla had told me it only stayed up for a few days every couple of weeks. But finally I found it again and it was busting with activity.

I hesitated before entering it. Ugly creatures strolled from stand to stand, just like the fae would in Sun City's marketplace. It was quite disturbing to see them acting so normal. Some creatures were tall and wide and strong, others were small and weak, some seemed old, others looked quite young, and most of them had a hint of mythical. Of magic. Either they possessed it, or they were touched by it.

I had never seen so many different races in one place.

As I walked into the marketplace, the creatures noticed my presence. They either recognized the cloak and wondered what a stranger was doing with Bloodwrath's cloak, or they were wondering about the stranger part.

Not in the mood to waste my time here or pick any fights, I kept the hood drawn and my head low, but my vision was sharp and I scanned the crowd for anything that could be helpful.

I didn't find any clues, but I did see something that made me stop in my tracks.

A young female fae.

A young female fae who had shackles around her wrists and ankles.

Her dark red hair was dirty, as was her fair skin, and bruises marred her face and arms.

I clenched my fists.

Who had the audacity to enslave a fae?

A rage I had felt only a handful of times took possession of me, and before I knew it, I was stalking to her.

The young fae saw me coming and turned her back to me, pretending to browse a stand displaying an array of colorful fabrics.

"You're fae," I said, my voice low. "You're a slave."

She shrugged one shoulder and turned away from me a little more. "Don't."

"Don't what?" I looked around. Despite the attention I had gotten when I first entered the marketplace, everyone seemed to have forgotten about me. "Don't free you? That's exactly what I plan to do."

"You don't know what you're doing."

"Of course I do," I insisted. Why was she acting this way? Why didn't she want to be freed? Was she so afraid of her captor? I could deal with him, whoever he was. "Have you heard of Bloodwrath?"

Slowly, she glanced at me over her shoulder, her eyes wide with both fear and curiosity. "Yes."

"I know her," I told her. "She's not as bad as they say. She's going to help me go back to Wyth." At least, I hoped she would. If she didn't, I would convince her to. "You can come with me. We can go back home and return to our lives."

The fear in her gaze disappeared, replaced by longing. "I …" She inhaled deeply. "I want to, but I shouldn't."

"Why not? We can plan everything. When we're ready, I'll come for you."

"You can't," she whispered.

"Then you come to us. You can come to the witch's cottage. It's located just southwest of here, deep into the forest, behind a thick thorn hedge. And if you—"

A shadow fell over me. I looked up and saw a big greenish creature baring his long teeth at me. He said something in another language, his words sharp and angry.

The female fae scurried behind him and hid herself around his legs.

So this was her captor.

Around us, everyone paused whatever they were doing. Most creatures seemed to be hiding from this ugly monster too. Was he so evil that even the others were afraid of him?

The ugly monster spoke again, his words harsher.

"He's asking what you want," the girl translated, her voice low and shaking.

"Nothing," I snapped, my eyes glued to the ugly creature's. "For now."

Knowing I had lost this round, I whirled on my heels and stomped away.

IF IT WEREN'T for the fae and the ugly monster, I would have stayed in the marketplace longer, searching for clues and magical items that could help Layla and me on our quest.

Well, *my* quest. But I would bring her on board soon enough.

But I didn't want to put the fae's life at risk, so I upped and left.

On my way back to the cottage, I kept thinking ... what else could I do? What else could I try? But I didn't know this land well. I didn't know what or who could help us. I didn't want to give up. Not yet.

Never.

I had to get back home.

I didn't notice the large tracks and the upturned earth, as if something had been dragged across the ground, until I was well into Layla's estate. But I froze when I saw the broken bench, most of the herb garden flattened, and an upturned bowl beside it, the contents scattered across the ground.

What in the scorching sun happened here?

Something moved behind me and I turned, a bolt of fire ready in my hands.

An ogre ducked under the cottage's door and exited to the porch. He wasn't as big as the others who had captured me before, but he looked strong just the same.

"Where's Layla?" I barked in fae language, but repeated the question in the human language I had heard the ogres speaking. "What have you done with her?"

"We have her," the ogre said, his voice rough around the foreign words. "If you want her to live, you'll come with me."

I frowned.

Yes, I wanted her alive, but I wouldn't go back like a scared cat.

I let go of my fire and extended my hands to the ogre. "Take me."

The ogre walked toward me. When he was away from the

cottage and in the middle of the garden, I waved my hands fast. A circle of fire appeared around him, high and strong. It twisted around him like a tornado, sucking all the air and moisture, and toasting him in place.

His terrible screams echoed in the air.

When I was certain he was dead, I let go of my magic. His charred body fell to the ground and became pure ashes.

Right now, I was out of compassion.

Without wasting a second, I ran toward the ogres' lands.

14

"CAN I HAVE SOME WATER?" I asked, just out of spite. I wasn't thirsty, not yet, but I hated being like this.

I tried rolling my shoulders again, but that only made my arms, which had been pulled behind me, ache more and the rope around my wrists to dig deeper into the skin. My knees hurt from kneeling on the floor, even with the fur rug underneath them. I sat my ass on my feet and tried relaxing, but the ogres standing guard beside the wooden chairs in the room wouldn't let me.

I glanced around, trying to see if anyone had complied with my wishes, but no one in the large, round room moved an inch.

Ugh, I hated ogres.

It was funny really how they actually thought Prince Varian would come for me. I was sure he wouldn't. There was no reason to. I couldn't help him go back to Wyth, and I was nothing to him. If I died here, he could actually have my cottage and hide behind my reputation. He could spin a lie like he killed me. That was sure to give him a good reputation too.

I let out a long sigh.

But for now, we waited because the ogres didn't want to kill me yet.

A shadow snaked out of the corner of the large room, weaving its way toward me. I braced myself as the lich formed his human-like shadow figure right in front of me.

"You're in trouble," he said in his eerie voice.

I frowned. I didn't know much about liches other than that they acted as ghosts—they were specters tied to a place. They couldn't leave, they couldn't do harm or touch anyone, but they were creepy as hell.

"Just go away," I muttered, not in the mood to argue with a shadow.

The lich laughed, a hoarse sound so in contrast with its form. But to my relief, it melted to the floor and snaked away, disappearing in the darkness across the room.

Movement caught my attention and I turned my head to see two ogres parting and letting a small woman in a rough but fancy blue gown walk past them.

I stared at her in disbelief.

She halted before me and offered me a mug filled with water. "You asked for a drink?" I nodded, my eyes glued to her. Slowly, she brought the mug to my lips and helped me take two big gulps. She pulled back, but stood her ground. "Better?"

Finally, I found my voice. "Carlyn."

She had changed since the last time I had seen her. Her brown hair was now short and her skin was pale, as if she never went outside anymore. But she still had the same regal air about her, the same arrogance, as if the world should bow at her feet.

Well, in this case, she had the upper hand.

"Long time no see," she said, a hint of a smile on her lips. "Your reputation has grown by leaps and bounds. Everyone in this realm knows you and fears you."

I didn't care about that, not right now. "What about you? What are you doing here?" I glanced around, to the ogres who surrounded us. "Are you a prisoner here too? Are they forcing you to work for them?"

She let out a hollow chuckle. "Oh, no, nothing like that. I've been working with the ogres because I want to. I showed them how powerful I can be, and they gave me a place among their ranks. I'm actually in line with Ranzio, their leader. He doesn't do anything without my counsel."

I gaped at her. "That's what you've been doing all these years?" She nodded. She didn't look one bit confused or apologetic for working with the ogres. For having me as bait. "And the fae? What do you want with him?"

"That's a funny story." Carlyn started pacing in front of me. "The ogres have one of their bigger rituals coming up in a couple of weeks and they need a powerful being to sacrifice and eat during the ritual. When the fae stumbled in their way, the ogres knew he would make a good lamb, so to speak. You see, a couple of years ago, another powerful fae ended up here and they used him as a sacrifice. The ritual was a success, and the ogres believe the summer prince will do the same."

"Wait ... you know he's the prince of the Summer Court?"

"Of course," she said casually. "I remember him from when we were in the Spring Court. He had come with his mother. What's her name? Queen Nas-something ...

Anyway. He was pretty to look at. A handsome face is hard to forget."

I gulped, my throat dry despite the water I had just drunk. Carlyn and I had been through a lot together. Despite having gone our separate ways once we landed in this cursed land, we had lived through the same horrors before and after. Maybe, just maybe, I could reach her cold heart and warm it a little.

"Carlyn, for old time's sake, just ... just let me go. Just this once. The summer prince won't come. He barely knows me; he has no reason to come."

"Oh, but I think he will," she said, sounding sure. "And don't try to win me over reminiscing about old times. We weren't friends then; we're barely acquaintances now. There's nothing I want to remember from those days." She paused and looked up at the vaulted ceiling, as if seeing something I couldn't. "Even when the other fae fell into our hands and I held his medallion, I didn't feel the urge to go back to Wyth or to the witches' realm. There's nothing for me there."

I gasped. "You had a medallion? And you didn't leave this land?"

She shrugged. "The medallion is with Ranzio. He keeps it as a token of his power. And no, as you can see, I didn't. I was nothing back home. I was just one more witch. Here, I have a place. Here, I have a name. I have power. I'm one of the heads of the ogre clan. I have no desire to go back. Ever."

I let that sink in.

There was a medallion in this keep. All I had to do was find it and take it to Varian. Then, he could go back home. My goodness, now I hoped for a damn miracle and that I found a way of escaping from it. The stranger wouldn't come for me, but I could definitely take the medallion to him.

And he would go back home.

"If you say so," I muttered, ignoring Carlyn.

She snorted at me and strolled away, leaving me alone.

Alone but hopeful.

AGAIN, I got a little lost on my way to the ogres' keep. I hadn't come straight from there to Layla's cottage, and now I wasn't going straight either. But eventually, I found my way and sneaked close to the wall, careful with patrols or other guards.

Knowing now that I could use my magic anywhere in the keep except the dungeons, I enveloped myself with glamour and sneaked over the wall. I advanced slowly, hiding each time an ogre came close. Even though I had my glamour on, I wouldn't take any chances.

As I approached the main building, I saw a smaller building to the side. The two doors were wide open and I could see a wall full of weapons inside. A weaponry. My magic was my best fighting tool, but I could always use a sword, especially if a witch decided to numb my magic.

There were a handful of ogres coming in and out of the large weaponry, either returning or taking big axes and maces. I sneaked in and looked around until I found what was probably a dagger to them, but it was a nice one-and-a-half hand sword for me. The most important thing about this sword, though, was the fact that the blade was thick but sharp. It seemed like it could cut through the ogre skin.

I made my way to the main building. I climbed up the side of a rough pillar and crawled over the roof, until I found that opening I had seen before when I had been taken to Carlyn. For some reason, I was sure they were holding Layla there.

And I was right. I spied through the gap in the ceiling and saw Layla in the center of the room, her hands tied behind her, and her curls in a messy bunch around her shoulders.

She looked unharmed, but even so, a sudden protectiveness made my chest tight. I hated seeing her like this. I wanted to save her, to protect her, to take care of her.

The feeling caught me by surprise, but I pushed it aside. This wasn't the time to dwell on that. Now it was the time for action.

Ogres formed a wide circle around Layla, ready to attack me the moment I showed my face.

The oldest trick came to mind, but I hoped these ogres were dumb enough to fall for it. Using my stealth, I walked to the other side of the keep, far away from where Layla was being held, and used my magic. I started a magical fire that wouldn't be put out easily.

As I thought, shouts of warning sounded all over the keep and dozens of ogres rushed to the fire. Immediately, I turned around and returned to the other room. On my way there, I caught sight of Carlyn running after the ogres, toward the fire. I sped up, knowing she would be a little brighter than them and realize what was happening.

Which meant I didn't have much time.

Back at the window above the circular room, I found only

four ogres had stayed behind to watch Layla. Without wasting time, I jumped through the hole, landing in a crouch, and raised a wall of fire around Layla and me.

The ogres shouted and Layla lifted her head, staring at me with wide eyes. "You're here."

I frowned. What? She thought I wouldn't come? "I'm here," I said, going for her chains. They were enchanted, of course, but with the mix of my fire and the sword I had stolen from the ogres, I was able to break the links. The charm over Layla fell instantly, and even I felt the magic rippling around her as she summoned it.

I opened a path with the fire, creating a corridor toward the closest exit.

Layla held on to my arm. "Wait."

I looked at her, confused. "Wait?"

"They have a medallion," she told me, her voice low. "Carlyn said Ranzio, their leader, has a medallion."

My breath caught. By the scorching heat, a medallion! I stared into Layla's blue eyes, seeing in them exactly what she was proposing—that we steal it.

I wanted to ...

But a moment later, loud footsteps and the clank of weapons echoed through the room as the ogres filled the room. I hesitated. For a moment, all I wanted was to fight these monsters and find the cursed medallion, but even I knew that was suicide. Besides, I was here to rescue Layla, not put her at more risk.

"Live to fight another day," I whispered. Layla stared at me, in disbelief, but I ignored her. I clutched her hand in mine and tugged her toward the exit.

We would have to fight our way out, but we could do it.

We could take down a handful of ogres and then make a run for it.

I controlled the fire corridor, keeping the hungry ogres back as Layla and I rushed to the exit.

And then Carlyn stepped right in our path.

16

LAYLA

"WHERE ARE YOUR MANNERS?" Carlyn asked, sugar lacing each one of her words. "Leaving without saying goodbye?" She tsked, shaking her head. "That's not very polite."

Monologuing in the middle of a fight like an evil tyrant? Carlyn had definitely changed.

I sent my magic to my fingertips. "Get out of our way, Carlyn."

She leaned forward and smiled. "Or what?"

That was it. Despite the exhaustion that took over every inch of my body, the pain in my wrists and arms, and the dizziness that threatened to send me under, I threw my hand out and sent a black bolt directly at her chest. She gasped and stepped to the side, deflecting it. Oh, so she hadn't been expecting me to attack?

I threw one bolt after the other, forcing her to step back. Meanwhile, Varian controlled his fire, keeping it up and around the ogres, making a path for us to leave this room.

When we were a couple of feet from Carlyn and the exit,

she finally recovered and raised a barrier of magic in front of her. My bolts died upon contact.

With a shout, Carlyn burst her shield into a million pieces and sent it toward us, like shards of glass. Varian pulled at my hand and sprinted out of the room. The moment we stepped outside, the fire raged higher and stronger.

We were halfway to the outer wall when an explosion shook the ground.

My steps faltered and I glanced back, shocked. Had the explosion killed them all?

As if reading my thoughts, Varian said, "I can feel the witch's power. She's somehow containing my fire, even with the explosion." I nodded, letting out a small sigh of relief. I probably shouldn't care about her after all of this, but Carlyn was a part of my past. I didn't wish her dead. Varian tugged at my hand again. "Let's go."

Pushing thoughts of Carlyn and the ogres out of my mind, I turned to Varian and let him guide us away from the ogres' fortress.

"WAIT," I said to Varian once we crossed onto my estate. "I want to ward this place." I dropped his arm, which I had been holding for balance and strength—he did run faster than me—and spun around. Dizziness rushed through me and I stumbled forward.

Varian caught my arm before I could fall on my face. "Careful." He kept me steady. "You're weak and hurt. You need to rest."

I pulled my arm free from his grip. "No, I need to do this; otherwise, they'll come after us and we'll be defenseless."

We could also leave my cottage and hide in the forest, but that meant we would be open to more predators and monsters, and I wasn't sure we could handle another fight right now.

Varian clenched his jaw, but nodded. "I'll stay here while you do it."

And he did. He stayed a step behind me while I tripped my way along the border of my land and created a magical wall around it. If the ogres came, it wouldn't stop them forever, but it would hold up long enough to warn me so we could escape.

"Done," I finally said, lowering my arms and as the energy was sucked from my body.

Varian grabbed my arm and hooked it around his broad shoulders. He practically carried me all the way to the cottage, and sat me in one of the chairs in the kitchen.

Without a word, he heated up some porridge and prepared some tea. "What do I put in it for healing?" he asked, glancing at me as his hands hovered over my grand array of herbs.

I fought a smile. "Bay leaf, carnation, agrimony, sage, and mint. These will help with healing and bring back my energy."

He snorted. "Sounds like magic."

"Well, it kind of is."

He glanced at me again, his golden-green eyes hooded, but visibly concerned. No, I was dizzy and weak and was imagining things.

"Here you go." Varian pushed a bowl of porridge on the table toward me and handed me a mug of tea.

I took it from him and inhaled the sweet scent deeply. The aroma already tickled my senses and made me more energized. I blew on it before drinking. One sip and I let out a relieved sigh as I felt my energy coming back to me.

"Thanks," I said before taking another long sip of the tea.

Varian pulled up a chair close to me. "You're welcome." Although he had set a plate of porridge for himself on the table, he didn't pay attention to it. He was looking at me, his gaze examining me.

"What?" I asked, looking down at myself.

I was a little dirty from being dragged through the forest, my wrists were bruised from the ropes, and my hair was a mess from the fight, but did I look so hideous he couldn't stop staring at me?

"I was worried," he muttered.

I blinked at him. "Of course, you still think I'm the only way you have of getting out of here. But I'm not. You shouldn't have come for me."

His brows curled down. "And leave you there to fend for yourself? You were taken because of me. Of course I had to come."

I took another long gulp of my tea. I already felt much better. "You're a fool." I remembered the medallion. I had told him about the medallion during the fight, and we had left it there. I was still mad at him for coming for me, but now I was madder that the medallion had been in our grasp and we had lost it. "And we're fools for leaving without the medallion."

"If we had stayed, we would either be captured or dead."

I knew he was right, but now we were back to square zero.

Well, that was not true. We now knew Ranzio, the leader of the ogres, had a fae medallion. All we had to do was come up with a plan to steal it.

So easy.

Varian handed me a damp rag, and I used it to clean my

hands and face. When I finished, I drank a little more of the magical tea. I rolled my shoulders and groaned as pain ricocheted down my arms and back. Being tied down had left me sorer than fighting.

Varian's eyes widened and he reached for me. "What is it? Are you hurt?" He took my hand in his and gently turned it, looking for injures on my arms. "I don't see anything." He moved his hands up my arms and cradled my neck, turning my face to one side and then the other. "You're fine. Aren't you?"

I had lost all words. All I could do was stare at him, at how close he was, at the warmth of his fingers on my skin, at the strength radiating from his body, now only inches from mine. My knees were between his, my bare feet touching his booted ones.

Despite being almost as dirty and sweaty as I was, Varian's scent enticed me. A mix of sand and heat and sea salt. I inhaled deeply, taking more of it into my lungs, letting it flood my senses.

The summer prince was quite handsome, and for some inexplicable reason, I wanted to kiss him.

Varian's eyes searched mine. As if he had read my thoughts, Varian's fingers dug into the nape of my neck gently, pulling me toward him, and he leaned into me. His lips were half an inch from mine when I felt it.

I gasped and pulled back.

"That was—"

With his hands frozen in the air between us, Varian nodded. "The mating call."

It had been as fast as lightning and struck right into my core. A pulsing, burning feeling that touched every cell of my body and fueled a deep desire in my heart.

I shook my head. I shouldn't have known what this was. I shouldn't have felt it. Witches didn't have mates. But fae did.

"I'm ..." I couldn't say it.

"You're my mate," Varian said, his tone a mix of awe and shock.

"It doesn't make sense."

Slowly, Varian took my hands in his again. My mind told me to pull back, but my heart didn't. Instead, my heart told me to hold on tight.

"I know it doesn't," he said, his eyes locked on mine. "I know you're scared. I am scared too. I hadn't really thought about mating, and the last thing I expected was to find my mate in a strange land." He entwined his fingers with mine. Holy shit, my hand fit his perfectly. As if it was made for it. And perhaps it was. "But now I have found you and I'm glad I did."

I shook my head, still struggling with my reasoning and my feelings. "This doesn't make sense."

"Stop fighting it, Layla." Varian tugged at my hands. "Just surrender."

17

VARIAN

Mating was such a normal thing in the fae world; it was expected. Anticipated.

I hadn't given much thought to mating before. I knew that when my time came, it would simply happen. I hadn't worried about it.

I just never thought it would happen outside of Wyth and with a non-fae woman.

Any reservation I had about Layla, any doubt I had of her helping me or trusting her flew out the window. Right now, all that mattered was that she was here with me, unharmed and looking especially sexy even with her messy hair and dirty clothes.

Afraid of going too fast and scaring her, I gently tugged at her hands, pulling her to me. "Surrender to me," I whispered.

Layla let out a short gasp, but didn't fight it anymore. When I pulled at her again, she came to me. I dropped one of her hands and reached for her, my fingers cupping her face as her lips met mine.

I inhaled deeply, taking in her scent and everything else,

as I closed my mouth around hers, as she opened her lips to me, and let me in. Just this ... just this kiss, just her lips, it was all amazing, intoxicating.

I deepened the kiss, needing more of her, and she melted into me. Without hesitation, I snaked my arms around her back and pulled her to me. She scooted out of her chair and into my lap, straddling me. I groaned as her hips rubbed mine, making my cock harder and harder by the second.

I slipped my hands down to her ass and tugged her even closer, so she could feel it all, so she could know how badly I wanted her. She let out a moan against my lips and squirmed over me, pushing even harder on me.

By the scorching heat ...

In one swift move, I held onto her waist and stood up, holding her tight to me. Without breaking the kiss, I set her on top of the kitchen table and stood between her legs. Her nails ran up and down my shoulder blades, making me shiver. I slipped one of my hands under her skirt, running my fingers up her smooth leg. When my fingers grazed her inner thigh, Layla tensed and pulled back an inch, breaking the kiss.

"Varian ..." she started, her cheeks suddenly red. "You should know, um, I've never—" She pressed her lips tight.

Then it hit me. She had come to this land young and alone. She was still a virgin. "It's okay," I said. "I understand." I cupped her face and showed her a small smile. "Don't worry. I'll take good care of you."

Without hesitation, I knelt in front of her and pushed her skirt up. Layla sucked in a sharp breath when I helped her out of her panties, without moving from the table, and then I stared at her core. She tried closing her legs, but I held her knees apart.

Slowly, I lowered myself to her, and flicked my tongue on her clitoris.

"Oh my gods," Layla whispered.

It was all the incentive I needed. I held on to her hips while I closed my mouth over her entrance and pleasured her. She trembled with each flick of my tongue, with each suck and rub. But she really lost it when I slipped one finger inside of her. Layla's hands closed around my hair, tugging it gently, holding me to her. I almost laughed, but I was too focused on giving her what she wanted. I slipped a second finger inside her and she cried out. She lay back on the table, pushing all the things on top of it aside, and I placed her knees on top of my shoulders, changing the angle, and pushing my fingers deeper.

"Oh, Varian," she said in a hoarse whisper. Hearing her call my name like that? I almost lost it right there. Instead, I pushed my fingers harder inside of her, and ran my tongue over her clit hard and fast.

Her hands stilled in my hair and a moment later her entire body broke down in trembles as she came. I continued my onslaught until the trembling lessened, but I didn't wait until it went away.

I stood and took off my clothes, then I closed my hands around her hips and pulled her to the edge of the table. I brought my cock to her core and very, very slowly, entered her.

"Oh my gods," she whispered again.

Her walls were tight and wet, and they pressed around my cock in a way I had never felt before. By the blazing sun, if this was what it meant to be inside of her, I wouldn't last long.

I went in until I couldn't any farther and then I stilled, letting her get used to me.

Layla propped herself on her elbows and looked at me. "Are you just going to stay there?" she asked, with a naughty voice.

"Scorching heat, no," I said with a laugh.

My chest swelled with desire and pride and everything else. I held on to her and started moving in and out, in and out. Slowly at first, getting used to this perfect sensation of being inside of her, but then I couldn't help it anymore. She felt good, she smelled good, she looked good. With each stroke, I moved faster and deeper, and Layla's moans got louder.

No, I didn't want to end it yet, not like this.

Knowing I wouldn't be able to hold on much longer, I pulled her torso up and held her in my arms, the both of us still connected, and took her to her bed. I sat her down on the thin mattress and helped her remove her dress.

Again, her cheeks gained that red tint that drove me crazy.

I ran my hands over her arms, up her stomach, around her breasts. By the blazing sun, she was gorgeous and soft and delicate and everything I wanted.

Slowly, I pushed her back in bed and lay on top of her, covering her body with mine. She exhaled softly and wrapped her arms around my shoulders, drawing me closer.

I started moving again, savoring the way our skin rubbed together, how her breasts pressed against my chest, how she tilted her head up and half-closed her eyes, lost in the sensation.

I wanted to give this to her. I wanted to give her everything.

Intoxicated by Layla, I thrust into her, taking my cock deeper and deeper, going faster and harder ... I held on as much as I could, but when her walls tightened around me and her body started trembling again with a second climax, I was done for.

I thrust into her once more and came undone. I held her tight while we both rode the climax down, sheltered into a temporary bliss.

Never in my long life had I experienced something like this. This connection, this want, this desire. And I would do anything I could to make sure Layla understood what this—us—meant to me.

***

THE NEXT MORNING, I woke up expecting to not find Layla in bed with me. But to my surprise, she was tucked against my side, her head on my upper arm, her hand on my stomach, and her legs tangled around mine.

Besides having sex with her, this was the best feeling. Slowly, I turned to her, winding my arm behind her back and pulling her closer to me.

She groaned, but buried her face in my chest.

I placed a kiss on top of her head, still stunned by this turn of events. If I hadn't been sent here, if I hadn't ended up in this forsaken land, I would have never met my mate.

The circumstances might not be good, but right now, I was glad I was here.

"Good morning," I whispered.

Layla froze in my arms. Her eyes shot open and she tilted her head to look at me. A moment later, she pulled back. "Hm," she started, avoiding my eyes.

"No, wait." I locked my arms around her. "Don't leave. Talk to me."

She stopped fighting, but kept an inch between our bodies. "Um, I'm not leaving. I just ... I was going to get up to make breakfast."

I watched her. She was tense, recoiled into herself, and looking everywhere but at me. What the scorching sun was happening here? I thought that after last night, she had lowered her guard and let me in. She had accepted she was my mate, and now had no reason to run from me.

Letting out a long, steadying breath, I reminded myself that it was rare for witches to mate, and most of the time when it happened, it was with someone of another race, like with a fae, or a vampire, or a werewolf. She wasn't used to thinking about mating. She hadn't expected this. So, I needed to give her some space, to let her breathe and come to terms with this.

"All right," I forced out, dropping my arms from her body, even though all I wanted was to hold on tighter.

Trying to hide her nakedness from me, Layla scurried out of bed and into the bathing room.

I closed my eyes for a minute, trying to be patient.

That would be hard.

OH MY GODS, what the hell had happened?

After fleeing to the bathroom, I cleaned up, slipped into a green gown, and then dashed from the bedroom. All the while, I refused to let my mind go to the topic that was hovering over my head, pressing over my shoulders, filling every cell of my body.

Oh my gods, it couldn't be.

I had told Varian I was going to make us breakfast, but I couldn't. I needed space, I needed time, and I needed to be alone. So despite what had happened between us and despite knowing the ogres could come marching into my place at any moment, I went to my garden and busied myself with working on my herbs. Some had been destroyed yesterday when the ogres came, and I needed to fix it all.

But as much as I worked and got my body and my hands busy, my mind was another matter. And to make things hard, I sometimes spied a shadow walking by the windows of the cottage, a sign that Varian was still there. I hadn't imagined him. That this wasn't a dream.

That Varian was my mate.

I gulped.

Never in my entire life had I cared about mates. Even when I lived among the Spring Court fae, and had learned and seen mating bonds snapping into place, I never cared about it. It all sounded like some fairy tale I wouldn't be allowed to take part in.

Until now.

Until Varian showed up in this cursed land, came barging into my life, and ruined my peace.

My hands stilled over my herbs and I closed my eyes, inhaling deeply.

And there was last night ... my gods, I hadn't wanted to give in, but how could I not when that feeling, that pull that connected Varian and me, was so strong. It had been new and steady, and I had been too weak.

Heat bloomed over my cheeks and spread down my body.

I had come to this land too young. I hadn't had sex before, even though I'd had had opportunities. Now I wondered if that was the reason behind all that, a reason I hadn't known back then, but now was clear and right in front of me.

I opened my eyes and glanced at the cottage. Even now I could feel it, the invisible line connecting us, tugging me toward Varian.

Was this something I could fight? Was this something I could break?

Did I want to fight it? To break it?

And what would it mean if I didn't? What would happen to me? I couldn't just believe Varian and I would steal the medallion from the ogres, go to the Summer Court, and live happily ever after.

Now *that* was a fairy tale, and I didn't believe in them.

I busied myself with my garden again, though some herbs weren't salvageable and I would have to start over.

Footsteps echoed on the porch and then crunched over the grass, coming in my direction.

I steeled myself and looked up.

Varian stood outside the herb patch, his long hair damp, and holding a mug. "I brought more of yesterday's tea. It seemed to help you last night."

I stared at him for a second, at a loss. Gods, he was so handsome, so strong, so passionate. He was desperate to get home, back to his loving mother. He was a good son, a kind prince. Honorable.

My heart squeezed. I pushed down on the ground and stood up. Slowly, I approached him and took the mug. "Thanks."

"My pleasure," he said, a little guarded. After my behavior, I didn't blame him.

I took a swallow of the hot medicine. Its energy seeped into me and I felt even better, more energized. I drank a little more, while trying to find words. Finally, I lowered the mug and looked straight at him. "The ogres will be back. You should leave."

His strong brows curled down. "What about you?"

"I ... I'll hide too."

"But not with me?"

I didn't say anything. It was hard to when my mind and my heart were at odds. Varian crossed his arms, his chest puffing out. "I won't leave you to fend for yourself, no matter what you say. Even if you keep up this wall you erected between us, I won't leave you alone."

A long sigh escaped from my lips. I walked past him,

toward the cottage, and sat on the porch steps, the mug warm in my hands. Varian followed me but halted a couple of feet away.

"I don't know what you think of me, but let me tell you, it's a lot worse than that." I inhaled deeply, bracing myself to tell him all about me. "In my coven in the witch's realm, I was considered a mediocre witch. I didn't have any special powers, and I wasn't as ... vicious as most witches. My younger sister, Linde, was the same. We were always seen as outcasts and freaks, even within our coven." Varian's shoulders relaxed, but his frown deepened. "Then one witch rose through the ranks of our coven. Sanna was her name."

Varian sucked in a sharp breath. "What?"

I nodded. "Yes. Sanna. She was ruthless, powerful, but she was ambitious. Being in our coven was not enough for her. One day, she disappeared. At first, everyone wondered if she had died, or fled, or taken over another coven ... no one knew. Until a few years later when she showed up again, but this time, she didn't try to reclaim her place in our coven. Instead, she told us about a wondrous place she had found, that she was working side by side with a powerful king, and together they were building an even better place. She asked who wanted to join her." I looked down at my mug. "I hesitated, but Linde didn't. She was fourteen at the time; I was fifteen. I was glad to pass unnoticed, but she had always wanted more. When she offered herself to go with Sanna, I realized that if I didn't join her, I would probably never see my sister again, and she was the only family I had left, the only friend I had. So Linde, myself, and another dozen witches joined Sanna."

"Let me guess," Varian said. He took three steps toward the porch and sat down beside me. "Then you all ended up at the Spring Court."

I nodded again. "Vasant received us with open arms and showered us with gifts. We were placed in beautiful suites, we ate the best food, we were clothed in the most beautiful gowns. And everyone seemed to be in awe of us." I sighed. "Now, I know it wasn't awe. It was disgust and fear." I shook my head once and continued, "At first, it seemed like we were working for a better future. Sanna helped us improve our magic, to become more powerful witches, while Vasant made the Spring Court the best court Wyth had ever seen." I snorted. "It didn't take long for us to see it was all a lie. Vasant was an evil tyrant and Sanna was the mad witch behind him."

"What happened then?" Varian asked, his frown gone. Now his golden-green eyes shone with concern. "I'm guessing you didn't support them anymore."

"You're right," I said. "Some didn't care as long as they had power, but most of us didn't agree with what Vasant and Sanna were up to. But when we confronted her, Sanna locked us in a dungeon below the Evergreen Castle, one designed to hold witches." I drank the last of my tea and set the mug down beside me. "Sanna tried to intimate us until we obeyed her again, to force us to work with her, but most resisted her. Linde and me included. One day, three witches tried to escape when they were being served food. Sanna captured them and killed them right before our eyes. A lesson, she said, to anyone considering escaping again." I smoothed a hand on the faint marks around my wrists from yesterday. These were nothing compared to all I had suffered before. "It was scary, horrible, but Linde and I didn't give in. We wouldn't become evil witches; we would rather die in that dungeon."

"How did you escape?" Varian asked, his voice somber.

"I'll get to that," I said. "Not long after that, Sanna visited us with a small red stone she had set into a golden ring. She said it had been a gift from Vasant and she was eager to show us what she could do with it. She chose one witch, sat her down in the hallway between the cells so we all could see, and then she used the power of the stone. Sanna sucked out the witch's magic, absorbing it, until the witch was nothing but skin and bones. She died looking like a mummy." I shuddered, still remembering the fear and horror deep in my core.

Varian placed a hand over mine, holding it gently. I didn't fight it. "You don't need to continue if you don't want to."

"I want to," I said. I wanted to tell him, so he knew what a horrible background I came from. After inhaling deeply, I continued, "One day, Sanna brought us all to a large room where she said we had work to do. I think she wanted to see if we would crack under pressure; if by torturing us, by instilling fear in us, she could force us to join her again. There was a pentagram drawn on the floor. Once we entered the pentagram, we couldn't leave, not without Sanna breaking the seal. Still, she had many of Vasant's guards in the room as a precaution. Again, she chose a witch and sucked out her magic until she was dead, telling us that if we didn't do what she wanted, she would do the same to us. That was when another witch, one who had been hiding how powerful she was, stepped up." I looked at Varian. "Carlyn."

His eyes widened. "You mean ... the one with the ogres right now?"

I nodded. "Yes. She and I are from the same coven. Once we were recruited by Sanna, we became friends. Colleagues was more like it. We worked together. And when Sanna locked us up, Carlyn was with Linde and me. She was also afraid of Sanna's wrath." It all sounded like decades ago. "But that day, Carlyn had had it. She used her magic to break her chains and attack Sanna. She broke the pentagram's seal and a battle started." I shook my head, hating to remember those details. "In the end, Carlyn was able to snatch a medallion from one of the guards. She opened up a portal and we crossed it." I let out a shaking exhale. "Many witches died that day. Some still in the Spring Court, some in the new land we had crossed to. In her haste to get out of there, Carlyn had opened a portal to anywhere, and it led us here. But while the portal was open and we were crossing, Sanna and the guards were still attacking us. They snatched the medallion ... and Sanna wounded my sister." I closed my eyes for a moment. "Only five of us escaped through the portal. My sister died in my arms minutes after, and the other two died not long after. Only Carlyn and I survived. Lost in this cursed land without a medallion to leave."

"By the scorching sun," Varian muttered.

"After a huge argument, Carlyn upped and left. I thought she had died or was like me, hiding somewhere, trying to survive. Until I saw her working for the ogres ..." That was still hard to believe. After all we had been through, after fighting Sanna and her tyranny, Carlyn had become like our old hateful mentor.

"Sorry about all you went through." Varian squeezed my hand. "I'm sorry about your sister."

"I buried her just beyond those trees." I pointed toward the forest.

Varian nodded. "I've seen the grave."

The grave. Where my sister was buried. My little sister who had been too tough for her age, too bright, too damn young. My sister who had been killed by Sanna and died in my arms.

It was all my fault.

I pulled my hand from Varian and stood up, putting space between us. "So now you see, I'm not a good person. You don't want to get mixed up with me. I'll help you get the medallion and get back home, but that's it." I wiped my damp hands on my dress. "Then we're done."

HER PAST ... so many things made sense. How well she spoke the fae language. How she was so reserved and lonely, and wanted to be, as if this was her punishment for the bad things she had done.

But nothing in this was her fault. Layla had been lured by that wicked witch, promised a better life, a prosperous future. She ended up in a web of lies she couldn't escape. She did the best she could under the circumstances. She survived, she fought ... and besides being stuck in this forsaken land, she ended up losing the only person who mattered to her.

At first, when she mentioned Sanna's name, I froze. How the hell was she involved with that wicked witch? But she had been a victim. Vasant and Sanna were pure evil.

"Sanna was the one who sent me here," I said, suddenly convinced of one thing.

This whole thing hadn't been a coincidence. Maybe Sanna had no idea where she was sending me, or where Layla and the other witches had escaped too, but somehow, the gods had a hand in all of this, and they had sent me here to find Layla.

To find my mate.

To bring her home with me, to give her a chance to redeem herself, even if I didn't think she had anything to redeem herself for.

Layla's face paled. "W-what?"

"Things escalated with Vasant," I explained. "Did you know he wasn't the rightful king? He killed his older brother, and all of his nieces and nephews, so he could be the king."

Layla averted her eyes. "Yes. It was one of the reasons the witches and I regretted our decision to follow Sanna."

"Vasant figured out his brother had another child, a half-human he had hidden in the human world," I continued. "He went after her. There was a battle at the Evergreen Castle. My mother and I were there, along with kings and queens from the other courts. During the fight, Sanna poisoned my mother and opened a portal, sending me here."

Layla shook her head. "Such a treacherous bitch."

I almost chuckled at that comment. "I'm not sure exactly what happened after that, but I've had dreams of my mother and Mahaeru, back in the Sun City."

Layla frowned. "Mahaeru. Mahaera. Mahaere. I heard a lot about them while I was at the Spring Court, but I never saw them."

"They are ... something else," I said. There were no words to describe the goddesses. "Anyway, I see them in dreams, but I don't think they are dreams at all. I think it's a way for Mahaeru to show me what is happening there." I paused, still shaken by all of this. "Apparently, Vasant fell, and the rightful heir was instated as queen. But my mother is still in bad shape. The poison is quickly spreading through her body."

"That does sound like something Sanna would do. I'm sorry." Layla took a step closer to me. "And what about Sanna?"

"I heard she was killed during the battle, but I don't know how."

Layla snorted. "I find that hard to believe. Sanna wasn't stupid. If she saw a losing battle, she would have left before she went down with it." She glanced at the sky, the two suns illuminating her beautiful face. "No, I'm sure Sanna is still alive, hiding somewhere, biding her time."

I frowned. I didn't like to think that was true. I wanted that wicked witch dead and buried deep in the earth, somewhere she couldn't crawl out of again.

But I wouldn't argue about that with Layla. There was no need for us to worry about Sanna and her demise from here. Right now, we had to worry about stealing the medallion and getting out of here.

"What do we do now?" I asked, my voice soft.

Layla stared at me, her blue eyes brilliant and alert. "Now, we pack to leave this place because ogres will come." I was sure of that too. In fact, I didn't know why they hadn't come yet. "Meanwhile, we plan how to infiltrate their keep and steal the medallion."

There was so much more I wanted to do, so much more I wanted to say. And above all, I wanted her. I wanted to touch her, to pull her closer to me, to have her come to me and lay her head on my chest and ask for comfort, to rely on me.

But I knew it was too early for her, too quick.

As a fae, I was immortal, and I knew witches lived a lot longer than humans. Some became immortals too.

We had time.

In silence, I stood from the porch steps and went inside the cottage with her so we could pack.

BEING around Varian muddled my thoughts. Instead of focusing and thinking about the task at hand, I kept getting distracted and thinking about him.

About us.

I didn't like feeling that I had no choice. Being his mate was a done deal, and even if I ignored it, it wouldn't go away. It would hover over my head for the rest of my life.

Still, I felt incredibly attracted by him ... in every sense. He was handsome, hot, and he seemed to be kind and worried about his mother and his people. He had come for me when he didn't need to. He was strong and honorable.

I shook my head and shoved another tunic inside my leather satchel. This was not the time to worry about things I couldn't control. All I had to do for now was ignore this ... the mating, my feelings, the hot fae just outside this room.

I shook my head.

After packing my satchel, I walked out of my bedroom to go to the kitchen and pack some food, but Varian was already there. He was putting bread and fruit and nuts inside a basket, along with a jug with tea.

I stared at his back for a moment, still amused that this was my mate. This man, this fae prince was my mate.

All I had to do was surrender.

But did I want to surrender? I watched him some more. He had cleaned up well since the first time I had seen him, and last night I had seen all of him—heat spread over my cheeks—and he was beautiful. Powerful. Sexy. Intoxicating.

Right now, I was wondering how long I would be able to fight this before I lost control.

Slowly, I approached him. By now, he had to have sensed my presence, but he remained quiet, packing the food for us. I opened my mouth to tell him I would help him when a growl sounded from outside.

Varian dropped the basket on the kitchen counter and turned to me. "What was that?"

"I don't know," I muttered, though it could only be some monster from this cursed land. We were expecting the ogres, weren't we?

Varian ran outside and stopped short on the porch. I went after him, and halted by his side, my mouth hanging open and my eyes wide, staring at the figure standing in the middle of my garden.

"There you are," the troll said in the common tongue.

"Haijen? H-how did you find me?" I asked, confused. He shouldn't have known where I lived. Realizing I had asked the question in fae, so used to talking to Varian by now, I asked again in his language.

"I'm here for revenge." Haijen glanced to Varian. "A certain fae told my slave about your place. Said you two were leaving and she could come with you." His lips curled up and he showed off his long fangs. "I caught her trying to escape."

My heart sank. That female fae always reminded me of Linde, which was why I felt so drawn to her. Why I always felt so protective of her.

I steeled myself. "Where is she now?"

"Not dead ... yet," he replied with a snort. "But she got what she deserved. She won't make it through the night."

I clenched my fists.

"What is he saying?" Varian whispered to me.

"Nothing good," I whispered back. I should be mad at him for causing this, for telling the fae girl about my place, but I wasn't. I knew he had done it because of the goodness in his heart. He never intended for the girl to be caught and beaten. I lifted my chin and said to the troll, "Leave."

Haijen shook his big head. "Not before I kill you, Bloodwrath." He licked his lips, running his blue tongue over his tusks. "I came for you, but I guess I'll have a fae for dinner too."

As if I would let him kill us. "Leave before I make you," I warned again.

The troll let out a harsh laugh. "Make me? Little witch, you're nothing. I know your reputation is fake. I can take you easily. I should have done that a long time ago."

Then he lunged at me.

VARIAN

I BARELY HAD time to react.

Before the troll got to Layla, I shot a bolt of fire at him. Haijen twisted out of the way and changed course. He stopped just a few feet from us, his feet apart, his hands raised. Ready for a fight.

The troll snickered, showing off his huge, sharp teeth.

He said something in his tongue and laughed some more.

"He's amused about your magic," Layla explained, her voice low. "He thinks you'll make a nice meal."

"Tell him to shut up and fight," I snarled, calling my power. Fire enveloped my arms.

Eager to end this fight before it even started, I threw a stream of firebolts his way. They hit him on the shoulders, arms, and chest. The troll jerked with each one, taking half steps back, but when I lowered my arms, the troll smirked at me.

"His skin is too thick," Layla said. "Unless you put him inside a pit of fire, he won't burn."

"I can arrange for a pit of fire," I half-joked. If that was the only way to get rid of this monster, I would find a way to dig a pit big enough for him in no time. "How do we kill a troll?"

"It isn't easy." Layla raised her arms, her blue eyes turning black. A dark wind appeared from the sky and wrapped around Haijen. "This will only buy us a little time." Layla turned to me. "I only saw one troll killed before. It was done by another troll, who was equally strong. He ripped the troll's chest open and dug out his heart."

I scowled. "I bet we can't do that with our bare hands."

Layla shook her head. "And I don't have any swords or weapon strong enough to cut through his skin."

"What else can you tell me about him that will help?"

She shrugged. "There's nothing much. Other than being absolutely greedy, trolls are nasty and strong. Really hard to kill."

Greedy.

That gave me an idea.

I rushed inside the cottage and brought the sack with my things outside. I stood beside Layla and said, "Let go of your wind."

She frowned at me. "Why?"

"Just do it." Layla turned to the troll, but before she could command her wind, the troll cut through it on his own. He let out a roar and rushed at us. "Wait!" I called out.

The troll hesitated but stopped.

Layla said something to him in their language, and the troll replied back. "He wants to know what we're doing."

"I don't think I need any translation for this." I extended my arm, showing the sack to him. I turned the pouch over and dumped the contents into my other hand, my jewelry spreading over my palm. Five rings, two bracelets, and a thick necklace. I didn't like jewelry, but I had been attending a fancy ball when I was sent here. But the biggest prize of all didn't fall from the sack. I had to fish it from inside.

Layla gasped when I pulled out my crown. "What are you doing?"

The troll's eyes widened, shining with the greed Layla had mentioned. Slowly, I approached him. "All of these can be yours, but you have to leave us alone," I said. When Layla didn't translate, I told her to.

"This isn't right," she said to me.

"Layla, just do it," I insisted. She pressed her lips tight, but finally translated my words. I continued, "And he has to let that young female fae go too."

Haijen looked from the items in my hand to Layla, to me, back to the gold and jewels between us. If he was really greedy, this would be a hard bounty to refuse. Everything was made of pure gold with large diamonds and other precious gems. And my crown was the icing on the cake.

The troll said something, then swiped the items from me.

"He said he'll accept your terms," Layla said, her tone somber. "He'll release the fae too, though he can't guarantee she'll make it because of her injuries."

"We'll take care of her," I said, never taking my eyes from the troll.

Layla said something else to the troll, and he nodded once. Then slowly, he took a few steps back, until he was a good distance from us. When the forest was right at his back, he turned and ran.

Her fists clenched, Layla stomped toward me. "What the hell did you do?"

I turned to her. "What do you mean?"

"You just gave away all of those things because of me. Your crown! How could you?"

"I did what I had to do."

She punched my shoulder. "Do you think I don't know the crowns in the fae realm are passed through generations. That wasn't just expensive. That was a family heirloom! Sentimentally, it was priceless!"

I held her wrist gently, before she could punch me again, and leaned closer to her. "You're more important than my crown."

She groaned and jerked her arm free of my grip. "You're only saying that because some destiny crap told us we are mates, otherwise you would have never offered your *crown* for me!"

"Layla ..." I shook my head once. When would I make her see that this, us, whatever we had, was so much more than fate or destiny or the ties of a mating call? "You are more important to me than all my riches, but I won't force that upon you if you're not comfortable." I pressed the empty sack between my hands. "All I want is for you to give in a little. To give this, us, a chance. Then you'll see it too."

She groaned again, but instead of answering me or yelling at me, she stomped into the forest.

My instinct was to go after her; we had just been attacked by a troll who had left through a similar path, and there were ogres after our heads, but I stood my ground.

I wanted her to give us a chance, but before that happened I had to give her some space. I just hoped she realized what she meant to me before we died in this forsaken land.

22

I DIDN'T GO FAR. All I needed was some space from the summer prince. A little fresh air to clear my head and let go of my frustration.

I couldn't control my thoughts though, and my mind wandered to what would have happened if Varian wasn't my mate. If we hadn't found out about the bond yet. Would he have offered his damn crown for me if I had been a nobody?

Probably not.

I shook my head, still upset about it all.

I walked around a little, but ended up right where I always did.

In front of Linde's grave.

I knelt beside the rough wooden plaque I had made and placed a hand on the damp earth. Several feet underneath, my dear younger sister was buried. Dead before she had reached adulthood.

If only I could go back in time. If only I had insisted we didn't join Sanna. But who was I kidding? I had been tempted too, only I had been too shy and scared to do it on my own. When Linde showed interest, I didn't resist. I went with her.

Though I had spun this scenario in my head thousands of times already, I never saw a different outcome. No matter what, Linde and I would have followed Sanna to Wyth. And history would repeat itself.

I felt his presence before I heard him. Perhaps it was the mating bond making me aware of his presence, or the quietness of the woods and my senses tuned to this place.

"Sorry," he said, stopping a few feet behind me. "I just ... I was worried and wanted to make sure you're okay."

I nodded. In a way, I understood his feelings, because I was starting to feel them myself. If I was honest, I would say that since the first moment I heard about him, that I saw him in the ogre's dungeon, I had been worried about him too.

"Come here." I patted the ground next to me. "I want to show you something."

It took him a couple of seconds, but Varian moved. He took three long steps and knelt beside me.

Without looking at him, I reached into one of the corners of the grave and started digging.

"Layla?" Varian asked, his tone guarded.

I didn't answer. Instead, I kept digging the damp earth with my bare hands. A good foot in, I closed my hand around the leather pouch and pulled it up. I took one of Varian's hands in mine, not caring that I was getting him dirty too, and turned the pouch's content in his hand.

A golden ring with a large red stone.

Varian's eyes widened.

"This is the ring I told you about," I said, finally meeting his eyes. "The one Sanna used to absorb our powers and to create powerful magic."

"How do you have it?"

"When Sanna injured Linde, Linde had ahold of Sanna's hands and pulled the ring from Sanna's finger. Linde held on to the ring, and even though she was dying, she knew what the ring meant. What it could do. So she hid it in her pocket. Her last words were for me to hide it and never use it, because she was afraid I would turn evil like Sanna if I did." I inhaled deeply. "I tried not to use it, but I did. Twice. It was how I got my reputation here. If it hadn't been for this ring, I would probably have been dead years ago."

Varian turned the ring in his hand. "But you ended up hiding it anyway."

"I did, because the stone is powerful," I said. "I can feel it calling to me even now."

"And you're suggesting you use it to steal the medallion," he said. A small smile tugged at my lips. I knew he would understand my intentions without the need to voice them. I nodded. "Are you sure?" He reached for me and held my hand in his free one. "I don't want to see you battling with yourself because of this ring."

"I think it's our only chance," I whispered.

He squeezed my hand, somehow giving me strength through this touch. "Then let's do it."

IT WAS DEJA-VU.

Layla and I headed to the ogres' keep. We waited until the two relentless suns went down before I glamoured us and we sneaked in. We climbed over the wall and tiptoed around the weaponry, and only saw a handful of ogres. From what Layla told me about their hunts and bonfires and loud manners, the keep seemed quiet for this time of the evening.

Well, it made our job easier.

Layla and I tiptoed around a big ogre stationed at one of the side doors and entered the keep. We were careful with noises around the few patrols we encountered as we went around the keep, looking for Ranzio, the leader.

Knowing a little more about ogres than I did, Layla guided us to the back of the keep, where the leader's quarters were. And there he was, alone in a large room, seated at a throne-like chair in front of a fireplace that was easily three times my height.

My heartbeat sped up when I saw the glinting medallion hanging from his chest. So he wore the medallion like a prized possession? It didn't matter. I would cut off his head and take it ... and go back home.

Layla stopped outside the wide archway, frowning at the king. She shook her head at me once.

I mouthed, "No what?"

A force slammed my back and pushed me into the room. I scrambled forward, trying to keep my balance, and ended up skidding on the balls of my feet so I wouldn't fall. I grabbed Layla's arm when she tripped and kept her up.

The force stopped and we found us in the middle of the large room.

Ranzio rose from his chair, his incredible height towering over us. His lips stretched wider over a sharp-toothed smile, and his eyes gleamed as he watched us.

He said something in the common language.

Layla groaned and called on her magic. Following her lead, I did the same and fire enveloped my hands.

"That would be a waste of time," a new voice echoed through the room, speaking in English. A moment later, Carlyn strolled into the room. "What took you so long? We've been waiting for you."

Before we could react, a curtain of foreign magic fell over the room and dozens of ogres filed in behind Carlyn, surrounding us.

"You ..." Layla started.

"What?" Carlyn snapped, halting a few feet from us. "Didn't you wonder why we didn't go after you?" She leaned closer. "Because I knew you would be back for the medallion."

Layla gasped. "It was a trap."

"Indeed." Carlyn's smile widened. "It worked beautifully, didn't it?"

Ranzio huffed. He said something in the common language and Carlyn chuckled.

"What did he say?" I asked in a whisper.

"That he's pleased about not only getting the fae back, but also a powerful witch," Layla whispered back. "He thinks this year's festival will be the most powerful of all with the both of us serving as their dinner."

By the scorching heat!

A shadow weaved past the ogres, coming toward the center of the room. It hovered close to the floor, until it was right in front of Layla and me. I held on to my fire closer, not sure of what was happening.

The shadow took the shape of a dark ghost, and an eerie voice rang through the room. "I told you that you had no idea what trouble you had gotten yourself into."

Oh, the blazing lich from the dungeon.

Layla beat me to it and threw a black bolt of magic directly at it. The shadow yelped and dispersed into the air.

Carlyn tsked. "Shame that doesn't kill him. This place would be much better without that damn lich." She waved the air, as if fanning away smoke. "Where were we? Oh yeah. As you can see, there's no way out. You're outnumbered and powerless." She raised her hand, showing a symbol carved from wood.

"A charm," Layla said, answering the question in my head. "It'll numb our magic."

"And not hers?" I asked, loud enough for Carlyn to hear.

"It should," Layla said, her eyes on her former friend.

"It will." Carlyn nodded. "But then it'll be the two of you against a hundred ogres. No magic whatsoever. Hm, I think the ogres will win." She let out a bored sigh. "Surrender now and let's save ourselves a headache."

Layla glanced at me. I dipped my chin once, slowly. A corner of her lips tugged up.

"Sorry, Carlyn." Layla threw up her hands. "We won't surrender." The red stone on her finger gleamed bright and a powerful wave of magic rippled through the room.

Carlyn and most of the ogres skidded back several paces, some even toppled to the floor in a heap of ugly bodies.

The witch fell on her knees but didn't lose her composure. She stared at Layla with wide, dangerous eyes. "You have the ring."

Layla's smiled stretched some more. "I do."

"Ranzio, you must flee," Carlyn yelled.

The leader of the ogres turned toward the nearest exit. Oh, no, he wouldn't. I ran after him.

The battle started. Ogres came into my path, but I used my magic to create a fire corridor, pushing the other ogres back and isolating their leader. In the center of the room, Layla destroyed the wooden charm and Carlyn attacked her.

I almost hesitated, wanting to help, but I knew that Layla wasn't a damsel in distress. She had been alone and alive for many years in this blazing land. She could take care of herself.

I pushed my worry aside and focused on Ranzio.

He rushed to the door, but I spread my fire wider, creating a thick orange barrier. He wasn't going anywhere. The big, nasty ogre turned to me with rage in his eyes and a bite in his teeth. He growled.

I halted and fashioned my magic into a long, fiery blade in my hand. When the ogre lunged at me, I stepped to the side and swiped the fire blade, cutting through his chest.

Blood oozed from the burnt gap, smoke hafting along with it, and the monster fell on his knees. He clutched his chest, as if he could fix the damage I had done, but there was nothing to be done now. Before we had come in, Layla had given me a burst of power from the ring and now my magic was incomparable, even if only for a short time.

Not even an ogre could resist the brunt of my fire now.

The other ogres roared, trying to advance through the fire, but the ones who dared met a similar fate. Their bodies caught on fire immediately and they burned to a crisp in a matter of seconds.

Ignoring their shouts and yells, I stepped right beside their leader and reached down. I wrapped my hand around the medallion and yanked, ripping the crude leather cord from Ranzio's neck.

I straightened and stared at the medallion, still not believing it was right in my hand. There was a moment when I thought Carlyn had been joking when she told Layla about the medallion to provoke her, that this medallion was a fake. But no, it wasn't. I could feel the familiar magic pulsing inside it. It was real. This was it.

I was going home.

I looked to the center of the room, but Layla and Carlyn weren't there. Instead, Layla had Carlyn backed into one of the corners in the room where the fire wasn't raging, a magical black dagger in her hand as Carlyn shook on her legs, eyes wide with fear.

Both of them looked like they had taken quite a beating with disheveled hair, bruises on their faces, and ripped sleeves, but in the end, Layla was stronger because of the stone in the ring.

But I knew she couldn't kill her former friend.

I walked to Layla and placed a gentle hand on her shoulder. "It's over." She startled and turned to me, brandishing the dagger. She realized it was me and put it down. "I have the medallion." I showed it to her. "We can leave now."

Her eyes widened and she lowered her hand. "We did it."

"We did," I whispered.

"No!" Carlyn let out a cry and rushed to Layla, her hands up and ready to do some damage.

I didn't think. I stepped into Layla's way and summoned my fiery blade. I extended it forward and Carlyn ran right into it. The fire plunged into her chest and spread like wildfire.

Beside me, Layla went still.

I extinguished the blade and Carlyn fell at our feet. Shocked by my actions, I turned to Layla. "I'm sorry."

Layla shook her head. "She wouldn't have stopped. You did what you to do." She glanced around the room, taking in the raging fire, the shrieking ogres, the many bodies thrashing on the floor. She shuddered, then glanced at me. "Let's get out of here."

"Let's." I extended my hand to her and she took it.

But as I clutched the medallion harder and opened the portal, two ogres broke through the fire and charged.

WE RUSHED through the portal and I almost fell face-first into white, hot sand.

"Watch out," Varian shouted.

I spun on my heels in time to see an ogre, who had crossed through the portal along with us, charging at me. There was another one behind him, zeroing in on Varian, but at least now the portal was closed.

I sidestepped the ogre and conjured a long shadow spear in my hand. When the ogre turned back toward me, I was ready for him. I plunged the spear into his chest. His thick skin resisted it, but I sent more magic into my shadow weapon and pushed it deep. It went through, piercing through the ogre's heart.

I let the spear dissolve into the air and the ogre fell at my feet.

I glanced at Varian and his opponent, who was running in circles, trying to extinguish the flames that covered his body. It took a minute, but finally, the ogre collapsed, quieting in the sand.

Varian was right in front of me. "I want to ... I'm sorry for Carlyn. I know you didn't want to kill her and—"

I shook my head. "I understand," I told him. "I know she wouldn't have stopped until she had locked us both up." To become the ogres' sacrifice during a damned ritual. She had gladly given my life away. I shouldn't bother with hers.

Her death would stay with me for a while, as all of the other witches' deaths would always be with me, but I would make my peace with it. Someday.

I inhaled deeply, resetting my racing heart, and took a good look around. All I could see was an endless ocean of sand and a big, yellow sun baking us from above.

"We're in the Summer Court, right?" I asked Varian. "You opened the portal to the right place?"

Varian came to stand by my side and nodded. "Yes, this is my kingdom. The Summer Court." Varian put a hand over his eyes and scanned the landscape. "There." He pointed to the east. I followed his direction, but didn't see anything. "There are some dried branches there. We can use those."

I squinted, but still didn't see anything. "For what?"

He gave me a small smile. "You'll see."

I LIFTED my chin up and felt the gentle, warm breeze brushing against my skin. Despite the heat, this wasn't bad.

Varian and I had walked until we reached the branches while he told me that small magical oases in the middle of the vast desert came and went every few years. This small gathering of dried trunks and broken branches happened to be one of those oases. I observed while he put a few bigger branches together and asked me to conjure a rope. He tied the branches together until they formed a long board, then told me to sit on them.

In no time, he used his summer prince powers and had us sailing—sandsailing—across the desert.

It was an ingenious way to move, I had to give him that.

But now that we were here, now that we were close to fulfilling his wish of coming back home, my gut tightened and my body filled with apprehension.

What would happen now?

Several times during our journey, I opened my mouth to ask him that same question but always ended up swallowing my words.

This was stupid. Why was I so afraid? I had to be practical. What would happen to me? To him? To us? He was the prince. He returned to his mother and his duty to protect his kingdom, but where did I fit in? Would he keep his promise to hand me the medallion and let me go?

Did I want to go?

"Var—" I finally gathered the courage to speak, but when the words started leaving my lips, the landscape changed in the distance.

First, it was a bright glow that burned my eyes if I looked at it too long. But then we got closer, the forms took shape. A large golden city sprawled around an equally large golden castle.

We were there. We had arrived in the Sun City.

MY HEART SQUEEZED at the sight in front of us.

The Sun City.

"Welcome to my home," I told Layla. I glanced at her, but she was staring at the city stretching as far as the eye could see. Though she had been to the Spring Court before, she had never come to the Summer Court, and here things were quite different.

The city's golden glint faded as we approached it, and instead the walls became a beige color with burnt-yellow roofs—thus the golden glow from the sunlight.

As I expected, the guards saw us coming from miles ahead and were waiting for us at the gates.

Once we were close enough, I stopped the sandsailer and jumped off.

"I can't believe my eyes," General Behar said as he walked toward us. The old man grabbed my arms and stared at me as if he was seeing a ghost. "Are you really here, my prince?"

I nodded, patting his shoulders. "It's me, general." I took a step to the side and gestured to Layla, who kept herself a few yards back, close to the sailer. I gestured for her to approach us, but she only took a small step. "This is Layla. She helped get me home."

General Behar looked at her, his eyes shining with pride. "Thank you, Lady Layla."

Layla, who hadn't been shy before, shrank into herself. She gave the general one curt nod, then glanced away.

I frowned, wondering what the problem was, though there was something else that deserved my immediate attention. I faced Behar again. "How's my mother?"

The general sucked in a sharp breath. "You better come and see, my prince."

THE RIDE through the city felt like a festive parade. Realizing their prince was back, the fae lined the streets. They cheered, waved, shouted, and clapped their hands, all thanking the gods that I had come home.

Seeing my people like this, together celebrating my return, warmed my heart. Now, if only I could save my mother.

My muscles contracted as we got closer to the palace. While riding through the city, General Behar told me about the poison spreading through my mother's body and the rebel uprising, determined to capture the throne. My dreams had been true, and all I could think about was that somehow Mahaeru had reached into my mind and sent those visions to me.

Once at the inner gates, I jumped off the horse and ran into the castle, barely paying attention to the shocked faces. Apparently, word of my arrival hadn't reached the palace yet.

I ran up the stairs and burst into my mother's chambers.

As I expected, Mahaeru stood beside my mother's bed. In her impassive and austere manner, the goddess looked at me, not one bit surprised to see me there.

"Finally," was all she said before glancing down at my mother again.

My heart skipped a bit at the sight. My strong mother, the queen of our kingdom, lay in bed with her dark skin pale and her face gaunt. She didn't look sick. She looked dead.

I took long steps toward her, dreading what I would find. Slowly, I knelt beside her and took her frail hand in mine. "Mother?"

My mother's eyes fluttered open. "Varian?" Her gaze widened at my face and her hand closed around mine, her grip too weak. "Is it really you? You're here?"

Tears filled my eyes. "Yes, mother, I'm here." I lowered my head to her hand and placed a kiss on her cold skin. "I'm here now."

My mother took in a ragged breath that rattled her chest. "Now I can rest in peace."

"No," Mahaeru said. "Not yet." She spun on her heels and walked to the door. She peeked out and said, "You. Come with me."

A moment later, Layla followed the goddess into the room, but she didn't dare approach us. Layla stayed by the door, her head low, her hands clasped together in front of herself.

I frowned, finding this image of her too different from her true personality. Why was she cowering like that?

"Who is this?" my mother asked, trying to sit up.

"This is a witch," Mahaeru said simply.

My mother's eyes widened some more. "W-what?"

"Don't worry, Queen Natsia," Mahaeru said. "Though she was one of Sanna's pets, she's not like the evil witch. In fact, I think she's here for a reason." Mahaeru gestured toward my mother. "Come, Layla. I know you can do it."

Layla stared at the goddess for a moment, then marched to the other side of my mother's bed. She sat at the edge of the mattress and reached for my mother. "Excuse me, Your Majesty."

She placed her hand over my mother's chest, the ring gleaming on her index finger, and closed her eyes. A dark light shone from underneath her hand. My mother sucked in a sharp breath and closed her eyes.

I tensed for a moment, but kept two things in mind: one, Layla was my mate. Even if she was reluctant to accept our feelings, she wouldn't willingly hurt me. And hurting my mother would be hurting me.

And two, Mahaeru wouldn't play with something like this.

A few tense minutes ticked by. At first, I thought nothing was happening, but then I saw it. The color returning to my mother's cheeks. The black mark on her neck dissolved. Her grip in mine tightened as her strength came back.

Layla opened her eyes and pulled her hand back. "It's done," she said. "You're fully healed, Queen Natsia."

A small, incredulous smile stretched over my mother's lips as she sat up in bed effortlessly. She glanced down at her chest, not believing the poison was gone.

"It's a miracle," she whispered, turning her eyes to my mate. "Thank you, Layla. How can I repay you? What reward can I give you?"

Layla stood from the bed and took a long step back. She

lowered her head and said, "That's not necessary, Your Majesty. I don't need anything."

"That's silly." My mother waved her off. "I insist we—"

I squeezed my mother's hand, pulling her attention to me. "It's okay, Mother. Layla said she doesn't want anything."

My mother tilted her head, sensing something. "We'll get back to that," she said to Layla, before returning her gaze to me. "As for you … I'm just glad you're here." She clasped my hand in hers. "While I was lying in this wretched bed, unable to go anywhere, I did a lot of thinking, and I've come to a decision."

I frowned. "About?"

"About you," she said, suddenly losing her amused and thankful smile. She grew serious, which meant business. "I've decided my time has come to an end, and yours should begin."

I blinked at her. "What do you mean?"

"I mean I'll pass the crown to you. You'll be king of the Summer Court."

I stared at my mother, sure I wasn't hearing her right. This had to be a joke. I glanced at Mahaeru, but she didn't even blink. The goddess knew about this. She approved of it.

I shook my head. "I'm not ready."

My mother patted my hand. "Nobody is ever ready for the crown, but I do know you're prepared. You'll be a wonderful king."

"But—"

She cut off my protest. "This is my will, Varian. Please accept it."

I swallowed hard.

I didn't want to accept it, not yet. My mother was immortal; she should be the queen for many more centuries. Why did she want to pass the crown to me? But I knew her. Once she came up with an idea, nothing could change her mind.

Well, I could accept it, but delay the coronation, couldn't I?

With that in my mind, I finally said, "All right. I accept."

26

MY HEART FILLED with something I hadn't felt in a long, long time.

Pride.

I was proud of Varian right now. He deserved the crown. I knew deep in my soul he would make a great king.

Slowly, I backed away from the bedroom. This was a tender moment between mother and son—and powerful goddess—and I didn't want to be the stranger interfering.

Besides, they looked so happy right now. So good. I couldn't stay near them for long or the darkness in my soul would taint them.

As I turned to leave the room, I heard the queen talking about hosting a huge ball to celebrate his return. And probably hold the coronation. They would decorate the entire castle and invite everyone in Wyth to attend.

I smiled as I walked away.

The guards didn't stop me when I crossed the archway leading to the vast, sand-colored hallways, or when I started down the beige marble stairs. This place was unreal with its round columns and intricate golden details. Such a beautiful, warm palace. Perfect for the Summer Court.

"Where do you think you're going?" an eerie voice filled the staircase and I turned halfway down to look up. But the voice wasn't coming from above. Frowning, I glanced around and found the goddess standing on the lower level, at the end of the stairs. I stared at her for a moment, in awe. She looked even more intimidating and powerful than before.

I had heard about the three mysterious goddesses of Wyth before. I never thought I would meet one of them face-to-face.

How did she just appear here so fast? Wasn't she just beside the queen? I shook my head. It didn't matter. She was a goddess after all. She probably could do things I couldn't even imagine.

"I don't know," I answer her frankly. "I was leaving the castle, going to the gardens. After that ..." I shrugged. "I would probably find someone willing to lend me a medallion so I could leave." Varian had the medallion we had stolen from the ogres, and I wasn't inclined to ask him to hand me that one. Though I had no idea where I would go. Back to the witches' realm? There was nothing for me there. To the human realm? I had been there once when I was younger. I wouldn't even know how to begin to live as a human.

There was nothing for me anywhere.

"You can't go yet," Mahaeru said.

My frown deepened. "Why not?"

"Because you have a purpose here."

I pointed up the stairs. "I just saved the queen. Wasn't that my purpose?"

Mahaeru shook her head. "No, you have a greater purpose here. Finish that, and then you can leave."

"I'm guessing you won't tell me what that purpose is so I can get this over with."

One corner of Mahaeru's lips turned up, but it wasn't a smile. It was a dare. "It'll find you instead."

Footsteps echoed from above the stairs, snatching my attention. I glanced up and saw Varian running down. When I faced forward again, the goddess was gone.

Of course. What kind of goddess would she be if she hadn't said something ominous and then left me here to mull over it by myself?

"There you are," Varian said, catching up to me. He halted by my side and instantly held my hand in his. "Where were you going?"

"I ..." I lowered my gaze, though I didn't have the heart to tell him what had been in my mind.

But he knew.

"You were leaving." He held on to my hand tighter. "Please don't leave. Not yet. Just ... give me a chance."

Maybe it was his words, his intense gaze on mine, the warmth from his touch, or the pull I felt even now connecting me to him. Or maybe it was Mahaeru's words and the curiosity they had drawn from me.

But I held the prince's stare and nodded. "I'll stay."

27

VARIAN

THE DAY WENT by too fast. I showed Layla to one of the largest guest chambers, not far from my own. I invited her to have dinner with my mother and me in our private dining room, but she refused, saying my mother probably wanted some time alone with me. Though I didn't think Layla was mistaken, I wanted her to join us. I wanted my mother to get to know her.

After all, she was my mate, and I was intent on making her stay.

During dinner with my mother, I almost told her about Layla, but decided I wouldn't until Layla was ready. My mother and I talked business: the upcoming ball, the coronation, and also about the rebel uprising. She hoped that now that I was back and she was well, they would soon settle down.

I hoped so, but had already made mental notes to talk to General Behar about it the next morning. Perhaps I should organize a party and go meet with these rebels, to show them I was here, to tell them face-to-face that my mother was well, and to listen to them. To understand why they were revolting against our government and do my best to be a fair leader.

As night fell and the agitation of my return faded, I grew restless. The image of Layla on the stairs sent a ripple through my heart even now. I had the feeling that if I hadn't gotten to her, she would have left. And that hurt. I knew that for some people, especially non-fae, the bond progressed slower, differently. I didn't expect her to love me right away. By the sun, I wasn't sure I loved her … not yet. But I felt a lot. I felt attracted to her, drawn to her. Just looking at her took my breath away. When she told me her story, when she showed me the hidden ring, when she healed my mother … it all filled me with immense pride. She made me proud. She made me feel worthy.

Worthy of maybe being the king I was supposed to be.

Worthy of her love.

Because of all these emotions swirling inside me, I couldn't sleep. Instead, I found myself getting up from my bed, putting on a thick robe over my naked shoulders, and leaving my chambers.

Before I knew it, I was standing in front of the closed doors to Layla's bedroom. Holding a breath, I knocked on the door and waited. A minute passed and there was no answer. It was still early, wasn't it? Was she already sleeping? Like a stalker, I pressed my ear to the door and listened. There was no sound coming from inside. I knocked again, suddenly worried about her, and again there was no answer.

Slowly, I turned the knob and pushed the door. I spied inside and called out, "Layla?"

My eyes went directly to the bed, but it was empty and the covers untouched. I frowned. Where was she? Light streamed from my left and I turned to it. The balcony doors were wide open, letting in the bright moonlight … and there she was.

My breath caught as I admired the vision before me.

Layla leaned her elbows over the stone railing, her chin on one of her hands, her head tilted toward the sky. She wore a white nightgown that reached her ankles, though the semi-translucent cloth left little to imagination. My muscles contracted and a rush of desire hit me like a whip. I kept telling myself I would give her time, but all I wanted right now was to have her under me again.

I approached her slowly, but even then, she jumped and gasped when she saw me. "What are you doing here?"

"Just came to check on you." I walked to her and halted when I reached the railing. I placed my hands on the rough stone and looked out at the Sun City glinting under the moonlight.

"Your city is beautiful," Layla said. "Your entire kingdom is."

I nodded. "It really is." I could stare at my city, at my king-dom, all day long. I could dive into its political and military and civilian problems with fervor and not come up for air for days—I knew that. I knew I was a dedicated prince. I just never thought I would suddenly be a king.

"What's going on in that head of yours?"

I shifted my gaze to Layla and found her staring intently at me. I let out a long breath and told her. "I confess I'm worried about being king."

Her delicate brows curled down. "Why?"

I shrugged. "I don't know … I never really considered it. In my mind, my mother was always the queen, and I was always her second." I ran a finger on the rough surface of the railing.

"The responsibility of caring for our kingdom was always hers. I was just there for support."

One corner of Layla's lips turned up. "You have to remember that you're the one who knows this kingdom the best. And your mother isn't going to abandon you, especially in the beginning. She'll take your role, supporting you." She reached out and placed a hand on my chest. I stilled. "You have a good heart, Varian. Follow that and you'll be a great king. The greatest of them all."

Almost in slow motion, I placed my hand over hers, pressing it against my chest, as if I could melt it in until it was holding my heart. She couldn't do that literally, but she still had it in her hands. She just didn't know it yet.

The small smile left her lips and her eyes rounded, the gleam in them flickering under the light of the moon. "You're beautiful," I whispered suddenly.

She didn't move. She didn't blink. Layla kept staring at me, but I could see the rise and fall of her chest speeding up. I wanted to reach out to her and feel her heartbeat too.

"Varian, I—"

Instinct took hold of me, and I erased the distance between us. I wrapped my arm around her waist and pulled her to me, making her words fade away. She stilled. "No, please, don't pull away from me." I leaned down until my forehead was touching hers. "Just ... stay where you are and let me come to you."

She let out a slow, measured breath. I thought she would pull away. Instead, she brought her other hand up and rested over my shoulder. "I'm trying to pull away, but it's much harder than I thought it would be," she admitted, her voice low.

"Why? Why are you trying to pull away?"

She shook her head and glanced up at my eyes. Our foreheads weren't touching anymore, but at least she remained in my arms. "I'm not the one you deserve."

I frowned. "That's not true ..." The words fell from my lips as a tiny point of light flickered in the distance. I straightened and looked over Layla's head to the desert in the distance, past the Sun City's sidewalls. "What is that?"

Layla spun in my arms and followed my gaze.

The light flickered again. Then another. And another. Slowly, a dozen faint lights appeared on the dark horizon. Then another dozen.

"Can you make out what it is?" Layla asked.

I shook my head. "Fae vision is good, but not that good."

"I can remedy that. Here." She placed two fingertips on my temple. A small rush of magic burst in my mind, and my vision enhanced in an instant. I now could see not only in the dark, but in the distance.

And what I saw made my heart sink and my stomach clench with dread.

I sucked in a sharp breath. "It's ... it's impossible."

"What is it?" she asked, her voice trembling with worry.

"It's ogres. We're under attack."

28

WHEN VARIAN and I first saw the lights in the desert, we thought the ogres were trying to keep hidden while approaching the city.

But we were wrong. The tallest ones climbed over the outer wall with ease, while the strongest used their brute force to bring parts of the wall down.

By the time Varian called General Behar and the army to defend his city, put on his armor, and stood at the top of the inner wall, the Sun City was ablaze with fire, screaming fae, and blood.

Even in the darkness of the night, the moonlight was enough to illuminate the horrors spreading in front of us.

While Varian changed into his armor, I had changed into some leather pants, a tunic, and a vest, something more practical for a battle.

For war.

A few feet from me, Varian barked orders at his generals and soldiers—evacuate the city, help the fae, kill the ogres. Several times, he started marching toward the gates, ready to join the fight, but his sensible mother, who had joined us in a full set of beautiful golden armor, had reasoned with him. He couldn't join the battle until things were more under control, or he would be lost too.

Every time the conversation steered that way, I pressed a hand to my stomach. I couldn't bear the thought of Varian in the middle of this carnage. Despite knowing Varian was a great warrior, I also knew this battle was mostly lost, at least for now. There were too many ogres, more than I had ever seen in one spot, and they were fighting dirty, violent, bloody.

At some point during the battle, Varian sent an elite group of warriors out to the city, tasked with the mission of controlling the fire spreading through the houses. All of them had extraordinary magical abilities and Varian was sure they could snuff out the fire in no time.

The battle was long and arduous, but finally, when the sun peeked in the horizon, bathing the sand in a golden ocean, it seemed the ogres had either been all killed or subdued.

Or so we thought.

Varian was ready to call victory when a second wave of ogres invaded the city ... and a woman led the attack.

The breath fled from my lungs. "Sanna," I whispered in disbelief.

"What?" Varian came to my side and looked out. "It can't be ..." He turned to his mother. "Isn't she dead?"

"I-I thought so," the queen stammered, clearly shocked. "If she escaped death, then she's even stronger than we first thought."

Varian had mentioned she had died, but I'd known it couldn't be. It wouldn't be easy to kill my former mentor.

Sanna and the ogres stopped in the middle of the main

road leading to the castle. Using her powers, she projected her voice so it was heard from afar. "Surprise!" She let out a loud cackle.

"I heard you were dead," I said, knowing very well that she could hear us.

"Right. About that," she started, sounding amused. "I know a losing battle when I see one. I escaped before it was too late."

"So you faked your death." As I had imagined.

"Well, that was convenient for me."

"So you could hide and plan how to make a comeback."

"Smart girl," she said, her voice purring. "I wonder who taught you those tricks."

I clenched my fists. She didn't teach me much more than to hate her. "What are you doing here?"

"What do you think? I'm here to visit an old friend." She snorted. "I had plans of stealing back the Spring Court, but when I heard you were back with the summer prince, hm, I couldn't resist."

"I'll give you one warning," I said, sounding a lot braver than I really was. "Turn around now. Leave and never show your face here again, or it'll be your end."

She didn't answer with words. Instead, she laughed so hard, she bent over and after a few seconds, she was out of breath.

With my magic, I raised an invisible shield in front of the inner wall, meant to keep the sounds away.

"I don't know why I just said that," I confessed to Varian. It wasn't like I could take Sanna head on.

"It's okay," he reassured me, briefly touching my hand. "I would have said the same thing."

"I agree, but how will we fight her? How will we defeat her?" the queen asked, more worried by the minute.

"We have numbers," Varian said, his voice fierce. "We'll overwhelm her, until she's too weak to continue."

It was a sound plan if Varian didn't mind losing good warriors in battle.

There had to be another way.

I glanced down at the ring in my hand. A sudden rush of clarity cut through me and I understood why Mahaeru said my time here hadn't ended. Because I had to defeat Sanna.

"I can take her," I whispered. Varian stilled beside me. "I'll use this ring for the last time to take her down." Then, I promised myself I would get rid of the damn ring and its magical stone somehow.

"Are you sure?" he asked, apprehensive.

I nodded. "Just keep the ogres busy while I fight her. Once she's down, I can subdue the ogres too."

Varian halted in front of me and took my hands in his. He fixed his eyes on mine and I could see the conflict in them as bright as the sunlight. But he didn't try to stop me. Instead he said, "I'll buy you as much time as I can."

29

VARIAN

MY FIRST INSTINCT was to hold on to Layla and tell her no. No, she wouldn't be going down to meet Sanna, of all creatures in this world. No, she wouldn't risk her life for me, for my kingdom ...

But at the same time, I knew her. She was strong and loyal and badass. If anyone could beat the wicked witch, it was my Layla. So, I pushed back my protective side and trusted her. I believed in her.

I knew she could do this.

Still, I felt my heart yanking as I took her down the inner wall so she could walk into what was sure to be the most fearsome battle of her life too—and possibly mine.

I wanted to give her armor, maybe a sword and shield, but she wouldn't need any of that. All she needed was the ring in her hand. The rest was theatrics.

I reached for her hands and laced my fingers with hers while I waited for my most elite warriors to arrive.

"Layla, I—" My words were caught off when someone suddenly stepped right by our side and caught our attention.

"Hold that thought," Mahaeru said. Where had she come from? How had she just appeared here? Elegant and stoic as always, the dark-haired goddess waved her hand and a large portal opened a few feet from us.

On instinct, I tugged Layla to me and took a large step back. "What are you doing?"

"I thought you could use some help." The goddess gestured to the portal.

Then familiar faces stepped through it: King Cadewyn and Queen Amber of the Winter Court, Queen Hayley and General Ashton of the Spring Court, and Prince Nox and Princess Amaya of the Night Court. Behind them, dozens of their soldiers marched out, filling the courtyard and mixing among my own soldiers.

But most surprising of all was the presence of Prince Redley of the Autumn Court. The Autumn Court had been quiet and isolated for so long, I sometimes forgot about them.

My jaw fell open. "What are you doing here?"

"Mahaeru told us you were back and needed some help," King Cadewyn said, clasping my arm. He wore his most elegant armor and his silver-white hair tied in a tight braid—his battle hairdo.

"I wouldn't miss a chance to take down Sanna," Queen Hayley said. She had a personal stake in this.

I glanced at them all, relieved. "Thank you for coming." I turned to Prince Redley, his dark hair tinted auburn under the sunlight. "I admit I'm surprised to see you." He held out my hand.

He grabbed my arm in a tight grip. "The Autumn Court has been quiet for too long."

I nodded, glad he was here. They all were here.

The walls shook with a new blast.

Layla slipped her hand in mine. "This is not the time for pleasantries," she said, her tone grave. "We better go before she reaches the gates."

I nodded, knowing she was right.

I brought her hand to my lips and kissed it, my eyes glued to hers. I hoped she could see how much she meant to me. But I couldn't dwell on it.

Instead, I let her go and turned to the warriors waiting for a command. I unsheathed my sword and shouted, "We destroy the ogres, and we rid our world of them!"

A roar met me, along with the bang of sword hilts and shields.

Without looking at Layla again, I marched out of the gates with my fellow warriors, and the real battle started. First, we cleared a path for Layla, but when she was in the line of sight of the wicked witch, I forced myself to turn my back to her and do what I had to—buy her time by keeping the ogres busy.

But I kept close in case she needed a hand.

I ran into the fray and started cutting through the ogres, imbuing my sword with my fire, and slowly whittling down their numbers. From the corner of my eye, I saw King Cadewyn tearing through the monsters' lines in his wolf form. General Ashton cut through our enemies with his sword as if they were made of smoke.

And then I saw Sanna throw a heavy boulder she had dug out of the ground toward Layla, who was already on her knees and panting. My heart squeezed, and I tried to get rid of the two ogres I was fighting to go to her.

An icy wind hit the boulder, changing its trajectory slightly, and vines sprouted from the ground, creating a net to catch it. To the side, Queen Amber and Queen Hayley switched between helping Layla and taking down ogres.

I felt immensely grateful.

The mace of an ogre hit me square in the shoulder and I flew a couple of feet, landing on my back on the hard ground. I groaned as I rolled to my feet before the mace squashed my chest. The ogre came at me with bared teeth and spit rolling down his mouth, and I pushed Layla out of my mind for now.

We fought against the ogres for what seemed hours, the sun was already on the other side of the horizon, starting to dip across the desert, and we had cleared a vast space.

I killed my hundredth ogre and raised my sword, ready for more. But there weren't many more. The ones I could see around me were already engaged in a fight with other warriors.

I made my way back to the real fight, which hadn't moved from the main road but had destroyed the pavement and pillars and porches along the way.

Even though she was breathing hard and sweating, Layla didn't stop. She threw bolt after bolt at Sanna, who seemed equally tired but equally powerful.

I wanted to go in and help, end this fast, but I knew this was something Layla had to do alone. I forced my feet to stay still and watched, my heart in my throat.

It didn't take long for Layla to break a thick sandstone pillar and throw the pieces at Sanna, a painful rain. The wicked witch waved her hand, sending most of the pieces to the side, but not all of them. The chunks hit her in the shoulder and legs, jerking her back.

But they had been a distraction. Once the pieces were gone, dark magic weaved around Sanna's legs and torso, holding her in place, and a spear appeared in front of Sanna's chest.

Slowly, Layla walked closer.

"It's over," she yelled, her voice hoarse with exhaustion.

"You can't imprison me!" Sanna yelled, shaking her body and trying to get rid of the magic. But it was the ring's magic. It was too powerful.

Layla shook her head. "I can't imprison you, because you would find a way to escape. Leaving you alive is too dangerous." Layla pressed her lips tight, and I could see this was hard for her, as hard as killing Carlyn or any other witch from her past would have been. "Goodbye, Sanna."

The spear forged ahead, piercing Sanna through the chest. The witch's eyes rounded and blood came out of her mouth.

Layla stepped even closer and closed her eyes. Light shone from Sanna's skin, and like a snake, it slithered away from her—white light at first, then black. Layla raised her hand and the light was sucked into the stone of the ring. Sanna's magic.

Without her magic, she was a frail human.

A moment later, Sanna's head lolled forward.

The wicked witch was dead.

Layla stumbled back several steps. I went to her, but Mahaeru beat me to it. Sensing the goddess's presence, Layla turned. In a flash, she slipped the ring off her finger and offered it to Mahaeru.

"Take this thing far away from me," she rasped.

Mahaeru took the ring. "You've done well." She glanced at me. "You both have."

I nodded at the goddess, but approached Layla. I halted a

foot from her, afraid of being too far away that she didn't know my feelings, or too close that she felt suffocated.

"I'm proud of you," I told her, with every fiber of my being. I knew it hadn't been easy for her to kill Sanna, but she had done it. For herself, for me, for my kingdom, and the fae realm. She finally avenged her sister. She was finally free.

"And I'm just tired." She leaned on me, resting her head on my chest.

The pride, the love, the protectiveness I felt for her spiked, and I wrapped my arms around her, keeping her close to me. I placed a kiss on the top of her head and whispered, "Everything will be fine now."

FOUR MONTHS LATER

LAYLA

IF IT HAD DEPENDED on me, I would have sat in the back. But since Varian asked so nicely, I was seated at the center of the first row, a few feet from the dais steps, where he was with his mother and Mahaeru.

Varian was able to delay his coronation for four months, but his mother wouldn't have it anymore. She knew he had been doing it on purpose, so she went ahead and organized everything. All Varian had to do was show up to his coronation.

My chest swelled with pride as I watched Mahaeru take the crown from Queen Natsia and placed it on Varian's head.

"I give you King Varian of the Summer Court," the goddess said, her voice ringing loud across the hall.

The guests clapped and cheered. Their contentment bled into me and I smiled wide with them, happy to share this moment with all of Wyth. Everyone had come for the occasion: King Cadewyn, Queen Amber, Queen Hayley, General Ashton, Prince Nox, Princess Amaya, and more. I was told

King Altan and Queen Zora of the Dawn Court had been invited, but they had been quiet since the last battle with Vasant, when they had surrendered to the evil fake king. The Dusk and the Day Courts sent a pair of nobles to represent them, and the Autumn Court hadn't answered the invitation. I had heard that they had been quiet for quite some time now, even though Prince Redley had shown up for the battle.

That was worrying to me since I had business with them. I glanced to my side, to where Willow stood—the young fae girl we had rescued from Haijen.

After we cleaned up the mess Sanna and the ogres had caused, Varian and I went back to that cursed realm. Varian took loads of gold and other precious items and traded all of those for Haijen's slaves and his crown back—he wouldn't wear that crown anymore, but there was still a sentimental value attached to it. Enchanted by the riches, Haijen didn't blink an eye. We sent the humans back to their realm and brought Willow with us. Now, we had to locate her family, which we assumed was the Autumn Court because of her hair color. Unfortunately, she didn't remember much about her life before, as she had been too young when she was taken, and according to Mahaera, who had examined her, her memories had been affected by the tragedy.

Speaking of Mahaera, I had finally met the other two goddesses. Mahaera had come to check on Willow first, but she had once also come to have tea with me—as if that was something a powerful goddess often did. And Mahaere had come twice to help me dress up for important occasions—the first official dinner I had with the nobles of the Summer Court, and for the coronation.

I was still not sure if the goddesses were three different

fae, or if they were one and the same. And when I asked, no one seemed to know the answer, or care for it.

After the cheers subsidized, Mahaeru guided Varian and his mother to the ballroom adjacent to the grand hall, where the party began. As expected, Varian stood at the edge of the dance floor, greeting his guests one by one. I went into the ballroom with Willow, but stayed to one side, happily taking in the sight.

Soon, the dance floor started filling up with couples dancing ... and Varian excused himself from the long line of guests still waiting to greet him and made his way to me.

"What are you doing?" I asked once he approached me.

"Taking my mate for a dance." He extended his hand to me. I stared at it for a moment. By now, everyone in Wyth knew we were mates. "Come."

"But the guests—"

"I'm king now and I do whatever I want. And right now, I want to dance with my beautiful mate."

I couldn't say no to that ...

With a smile, I slipped my hand in his and let him lead me to the dance floor. The other fae stopped and stared, some with smiles, some with curiosity written on their faces. It wasn't every day a fae mated with a witch, was it? Especially one who had been mentored by another witch, one who caused grief in the lives of so many of them.

I couldn't blame them if they were wary of me.

Varian halted in the center of the dance floor and turned to me. With a happy glint in his dark green eyes, he placed a possessive hand behind my back and pulled me to him.

I stared into his eyes, practically lost in them.

After the battle against Sanna, after killing her, I almost left. Again. Varian had been heartbroken when I mentioned it to him, but he had promised to do whatever I wanted, so even though he had unshed tears in his eyes, he handed me a medallion so I could leave.

But once I had the medallion in my hands, I realized I didn't want to leave. And it wasn't because there wasn't any other place or person waiting for me. It was because I didn't want to leave Varian.

Varian—my home. My mate.

I wanted to be wherever he was.

That was it.

Four months had passed since then, and despite the politics, which bored me to hell, life had been like a fairy tale. Queen Natsia had mentioned a wedding a handful of times since then, but I was happy the way we were right now.

One day, I would marry Varian. Why wouldn't I if I loved him? If he was my mate and I had no intentions of ever leaving him? But there was no need to rush that.

For now, I enjoyed his company, his touch, his smile, his hands on me one day at a time.

"I'm sorry you weren't by my side during the ceremony," he said, his tone serious.

I nodded. "It's okay." Mahaeru had explained it to me before. I was Varian's mate, but I wasn't his wife, which meant I wouldn't become queen and I shouldn't be a part of the ceremony as he was.

It made sense and I respected it. Honestly, I had no ambition to be a part of his kingdom, much less to be queen. The idea actually terrified me. When I voiced that to the goddess, she assured me it would grow on me, and I would happily become queen one day.

We would see about that.

"Did I tell you that you look beautiful tonight?" he said. Again.

I rolled my eyes. "Just three hundred times."

"But it's true. I mean, you're always beautiful, but there's something about you tonight ..." He bit down on his lower lip. "You know what? We're leaving." He promptly let go of me, to hold my hand tighter and march us out of the ballroom.

"Varian? What are you doing?"

He didn't say anything as he took me past the guards at the ballroom's entrance, through a long hallway, up the stairs, into the royal wing of the castle, and into his chambers—*our* chambers. I had moved in with him to this bedroom a couple of months ago and I was still not used to it.

"Less talking, more kissing," he whispered, turning to me. He kicked the door closed and pushed me against it, ripping a small gasp from my lips. He wrapped his hands around my wrists and brought my hands above my head. "I've been wanting to take off this dress since the moment I first saw you in it." He leaned into me and grazed his soft, soft lips across the skin of my neck.

"I thought you would like this dress," I whispered, slightly out of breath.

"Oh, I loved this dress." He pressed his hips on mine, pushing his hard-on against me. I gasped again. "I've been fighting this ever since." He brought his lips to my chin. "I don't want to fight it anymore."

Then his mouth was on mine and I was lost. Every time Varian put his hands on me, I lost ... I lost my mind, I lost control over my body, I lost everything. All that mattered was him, his body, his hands, his skin—all of him touching me.

In a matter of seconds, the dress was on the floor, forgotten.

Gentle as always, Varian picked me up and deposited me in our bed. Then he stepped back and stared at me, naked and exposed. Without breaking his hungry stare, he took off his fancy clothes, and then the hunger was inside me as well. The man was completely ripped, his dark golden skin smooth over the hundreds of muscles lining his entire body. He was perfection in every way, and he was mine. Only mine.

"Come here," I breathed.

One corner of his lips tugged up and he obliged. He covered my body with his warm one and I let out a satisfied sigh. How I loved when we were skin to skin, when he looked at me as if there was no one else in the world. I loved it all.

I loved him.

"I love you," I said, looking directly into his eyes. I had only said it once before, not long ago, and the words had felt foreign back then. I had known I loved him, but my mind was still not ready for all of what came with it. But now it was. I was finally willing to surrender my mind and soul to my handsome mate. "I really, really love you."

"Good," he said, holding my stare. "Because I really, really love you too."

He moved, aligning himself with me, and then he thrust forward, entering me in one swift move. I gasped out loud, holding on to his shoulders as if my life depended on it. "And I'll show you just how much right now." He started moving in and out, in and out, fast and hard, without mercy.

"I'm counting on it," I said, my voice breaking between moans.

Indeed he showed me, taking me to heights I hadn't imagined possible to reach. And the best part was that I was sure he would never let me come down.

This was our own kind of fairy tale, and I knew we had finally reached the happily ever after.

***

Extend your stay on The Wyth Courts by pre-ordering Autumn Rebel, book 4!

THANK YOU

Thank you for reading *Summer Prince*!

Reviews are very important for authors. If you liked my book, please consider leaving a review on your favorite online retailer and/or on goodreads, please!

Pre-order *Autumn Rebel (book 4)* now!

Don't get to sign up for my newsletter so you don't miss news about deals, new releases, cover reveals, and more!

If you want to see exclusive teasers, help me decide on covers, read excerpts, talk about books, etc, join my reader group on Facebook: Juliana's Club!

THE VAMPIRE HUNT

I have an **exclusive** novella set in the Rite World that is just for my newsletter subscribers!

Click here to sign-up and receive your book!

THE VAMPIRE HUNT
A Rite World Novella

Norah is a demon hunter, one of the best graduated from the Blackthorn Hunters Academy. When she's sent to investigate a case concerning demons in a small town, she runs into a very arrogant vampire. Her first instinct is to kill him, after all, he's a supernatural and demon hunters are taught to end all evil.

Cain is a vampire prince. Because of his status, he's in charge of making sure humans don't find out about his kind. During a routine investigation, he bumps into a very sexy demon hunter and he wonders what she's doing on his way.

However, the case grows much bigger for Norah and Cain to handle alone. To find the truth and win this battle, the vampire and the demon hunter will have to hunt together—without killing each other.

How well could this end?

ABOUT THE AUTHOR

While USA Today Bestselling Author Juliana Haygert dreams of being Wonder Woman, Buffy, or a blood elf shadow priest, she settles for the less exciting—but equally gratifying—life as a wife, a mother, and an author. She resides in North Carolina and spends her days writing about kick-ass heroines and the heroes who drive them crazy.

Subscribe to her mailing list to receive emails of announcement, events, and other fun stuff related to her writing and her books: www.bit.ly/JuHNL

For more information:
www.julianahaygert.com

facebook.com/julianahaygert

twitter.com/juliana_haygert

instagram.com/juliana.haygert

goodreads.com/juliana_haygert

pinterest.com/julianahaygert

bookbub.com/authors/juliana-haygert

ALSO BY JULIANA HAYGERT

To find links and more info, go to:

www.julianahaygert.com/books/

Shorts

Into the Darkest Fire

Rite World: Blackthorn Hunters Academy

The Demon Kiss (Book 1)

The Hunter Secret (Book 2)

The Soul Bond (Book 3)

The Shadow Trials (Book 4)

The Infernal Curse (Book 5)

Rite World

The Vampire Heir (Book 1)

The Witch Queen (Book 2)

The Immortal Vow (Book 3)

The Warlock Lord (Book 4)

The Wolf Consort (Book 5)

The Crystal Rose (Book 6)

The Wolf Forsaken (Book 7)

The Fae Bound (Book 8)

The Blood Pact (Book 9)

The Wyth Courts

Winter King (Book 1)

Spring Warrior (Book 2)

Summer Prince (Book 3)

Autumn Rebel (Book 4)

The Fire Heart Chronicles

Heart Seeker (Book 1)

Flame Caster (Book 2)

Sorrow Bringer (Book 3)

Earth Shaker (Novella)

Soul Wanderer (Book 4)

Fate Summoner (Book 5)

War Maiden (Book 6)

The Everlast Series

Destiny Gift (Book 1)

Soul Oath (Book 2)

Cup of Life (Book 3)

Everlasting Circle (Book 4)

Willow Harbor Series

Hunter's Revenge (Book 3)

Siren's Song (Book 5)

Breaking Series

Breaking Free (Book 1)

Breaking Away (Book 2)

Breaking Through (Book 3)

Breaking Down (Book 4)

Standalones

Daughter of Darkness